Born in the Caribbean, the author emigrated to England in the '60s where she trained and worked as a nurse and social worker, later studying at Sussex University and graduating with a B.A. Hons. in politics in 1984.

Writing, always being her secret ambition, some of her articles were published in Campus Newspaper, Church magazines and magazines in general.

But it was while she was working as a social worker, that her desire to explore social injustice deepened, hence her second novel, MERCY FARM.

Her first novel, BROWN SUGAR, published in 1996, was a 'sell out' and she is currently working on her third novel.

By the same author

BROWN SUGAR (first published 1996)
ISBN 978 1 56002 588 7

MERCY FARM

GAYLE HONEYCOMBE

MERCY FARM

Vanguard Press

A CIP catalogue record for this title is
available from the British Library.

ISBN 978 1 84386 348 9

**Any characters, societies and names and dates
of legal acts mentioned in this publication
are purely fictitious.**

*Vanguard Press is an imprint of
Pegasus Elliot MacKenzie Publishers Ltd.*
www.pegasuspublishers.com

First Published in 2007

**Vanguard Press
Sheraton House Castle Park
Cambridge England**

Printed & Bound in Great Britain

To my teachers Eunice and Harold
who taught me how to read and write.

CHAPTER ONE

Patsy sat at the cramped breakfast table and stared at the bowl of porridge in front of her, a sad tearful look on her face. "Huh, Huh! Huh, Huh!" she hollered, "Ah don'e wan' to go to scool today," and rocking her head from side to side, she pushed the bowl with such force that it skidded to the edge of the table and nearly landed on the floor.

Trixie sprung to her feet, quickly edged the bowl back in front of Patsy and tried to coax her into eating it. Scooping up a spoonful of porridge, she whispered. "Come on, 'ere we are," and slid the porridge gently into Patsy's mouth.

Patsy swallowed, then, "Huh, Huh! Huh, Huh!" she went, "Ah don'e wan to go to scool today," tears flooding her forlorn cheeks, as she protested. She pushed the bowl away again, with less force this time.

But Trixie was not going to give in. She placed the bowl firmly back in front of Patsy, mopped Patsy's eyes tentatively, then, scooping up some more porridge, she coaxed, "Come on, 'ere we are," and slid it gently into Patsy's mouth.

Patsy swallowed and was about to holler again, when, in her own motherly way, Trixie stopped her in her tracks.

"Sh-u-sh... Shu-u-sh! ..." she went, "sh-u-sh!..." she asserted, and all of a sudden, Patsy went quiet.

She was used to Patsy's childlike behaviour – monkey protest, monkey tears – but today she was not going to pamper to her whims. Today they were going to Hope Centre, Hope – where they would learn the art of survival, the art of living, the rule of the game.

It was and unwritten code – they had to attend. Any dodginess and there was hell to play, so she scooped and fed, until Patsy demolished the whole bowl of porridge and drank a full mug of tea. Then gingerly, she led her up to her room, washed and dressed her and by 8am they were ready and waiting for Hope's minibus to take them to Hope Centre.

Two strange women: Trixie whose tongue bobbed about her mouth and sometimes dribbled when she tried to speak, and Patsy with her childlike mannerisms, always drawling, protesting, crying monkey tears. Now, here they were, two weird women, waiting to take up their positions at a place they called Hope.

They were best friends. They shared a special brand of friendship; a camaraderie that was hard to understand; an unusual kind of bond; a bond that meant survival for them in that harsh and daunting world of Mercy Farm.

Josie the carer was astounded. She couldn't believe what her eyes were seeing. She stared in disbelief at the unforgotten scenes; scenes that unfolded like a haphazard, unwoven work of tapestry in front of her.

There they were – Two unlikely women – Trixie, 45, and Patsy almost 50, sharing their love, their compassion, their lives, without conditions. Then, there were Frankie and Jonnie, scheming, plotting, hatching the unmentionable, the unthinkable. As for the others, well they fitted in and out like a jigsaw puzzle – one with a difference.

Where she'd worked before, the elderly women were so cruel to each other – swearing, cursing, bitching about but never making a single move to help each other out. And Josie thought she'd seen the worst.

Now, here she was on this warm spring day, April 1989, watching a scene... the likes of which she had never seen before.

At last she'd found the right job, or so she thought...

CHAPTER TWO

At St Peter's hospital, Betty O'Connor laid on the labour couch for three hours, puffing, panting, and sweating.

Six other women also lay on couches along that corridor, shouting obscenities or simply screaming – they were all in labour – the little midwife and her assistant hovering around them like bees bustling for honey. And with just the odd screen for privacy, these women had almost become a free spectacle for any passer-by, as they lay there puffing and panting away.

Betty felt a griping pain in the small of her back and red hot pinchers churning somewhere inside her. Then pu-u-f! Her waters burst. She pushed and screamed, "Nurse, Nurse! It's coming, quick!" No one came.

At 45, with six children and high blood pressure, the district nurse had sent Betty into hospital to have her seventh baby because she was scared she would haemorrhage and die. And now, here she was, screaming, panting and heaving and no one came. She was terrified.

'Any moment now,' she thought, 'the baby will shoot out and fall off the narrow couch and no one will be there to save it.' She was petrified.

Then, the hot pain came again. She blew and pushed, "Nurse, Nurse, aah! It's come, Nurse... Nurse!..." and the baby shot out like a bullet from a charged gun, blood spurting all over the place, on the couch, on the floor, everywhere, it seemed. It was exactly 9am.

Like a flash, the midwife bolted towards her. "The trolley! The trolley!" she shouted. "Nurse! Bring the trolley, quick! Quick! Quick!" And suddenly, mayhem. Betty could hear the running of feet, crackling of starched uniforms, voices saying unintelligible words, as she laid there, tired, confused, half out of her mind.

Quickly, the midwife cut the baby's umbilical cord, held it up by its legs and sharply slapped its bottom. It made a faint, feeble cry. Then, with precision, she swabbed it and wrapped it in a towel. But by the look on her face and the whispering going on around her, Betty could tell that all was not well.

"Something wrong?" she hollered, half consciously.

"Oh, nothing wrong," the little Malaysian assistant replied. "You have a lovely baby girl," and… clutching the baby in her arms she scurried away to the nursery, the midwife having instructed her to phone the doctor instantly.

The Malaysian nurse had shot out the door as if a bolt of lightening had just struck her and Betty did not even get to see her newborn baby. She was certain something had gone awfully wrong. Then within minutes, she was wheeled to the maternity ward but she was too weak and too exhausted to ask any questions. She knew she would be fobbed off.

She laid there feeling empty, confused, cheated. 'They took her baby away and she didn't even get to see it, touch it, feel it, hear its heart beat,' she thought as waves of depression threatened to engulf her soul and crush her spirit. – And to make it worse, there was no one there to speak on her behalf.

All day long Dr Chan was busy. In and out of the Nursery, he scuttled, carrying out tests on the baby, phoning here, phoning there, ringing the various departments until he was pretty sure of the baby's diagnosis. Then, at 5pm, in his stiff white coat with a stethoscope dangling precariously from his neck, he made his way to Betty's bedside, with the midwife towing along behind him, carrying the baby.

"Good evening Mrs O'Connor, and how are you feeling now?"

"Not too bad Doctor," Betty replied (although she felt bad she couldn't say it – the words just spurted out of her mouth).

"Good, good, Mrs O'Connor," he blurted out. "I have news for you," the expression on his face changing and Betty could sense this. "Y-es, yes Doctor?" Betty quizzed nervously, suspecting something was wrong, but she wasn't sure. She hoped with all her heart that it would be good news.

"Mrs O'Connor, the baby..." (The contour on his face was changing so much he was almost distraught whilst the midwife on the other hand, kept a strong grip on the baby.)

Betty's eyes shot from him to the midwife and back again. "What do you mean Doctor?" she almost snapped, the pain gripping her head going round and round in circles, things wheeling in her mind.

"Mrs O'Connor, your baby is..." he hesitated.

"She's a Mongol dear, mentally retarded. She won't be able to do a thing dear," the midwife intercepted, tactlessly.

Betty felt a sickening thud in the pit of her stomach as she shook uncontrollably. Then she screamed, "Oh no, no no! It couldn't happen to me." Then... "Take her away, take her away! I don't want to see her!"

The tactless little midwife had done it all wrong. Now, all she could do was run as fast as her short bandy legs could carry her, clutching the little bundle in her arms.

Betty felt sick but nothing would come out, the distraught doctor standing there hopelessly trying to pacify her, but to no avail. He would come back later when she'd calmed down. 'Right now he must leave her to try and calm herself down. Right now he knew she just couldn't cope.'

And so Betty O'Connor was left all alone to try and cope with her soul-destroying emotions, the pain gripping like a sharp knife driving through her stomach, as she thought about the half-witted child she had just given birth to. Tom was doing his pub rounds as usual, drinking himself stupid. And now there was no one to turn to, no one to off-load her terrible burden onto.

She cried and cried until she fell asleep.

She had heard about Mongolism and when she woke up after only a few hours sleep it all began to come back to her –

slowly, slowly, it came... It was from her family, she remembered: rumours, gossip about her half-witted brother Stan, who died when she was barely two. And thank God, he being the 9th of her mother's ten children and she being the last, she was saved the plight of seeing him alive. And now, this...

Her mother Enid was also 45 when she gave birth to Stan and so all Betty could think of now was that God had put a curse on her. "Oh God, it's a curse, it's a curse. Spare me God, spare me."

She didn't know about Trisomy 21, the extra chromosome 21 which did not separate from its partner during conception. It tended to happen in women aged 45 or so, as their ageing cells were more likely to be unstable. The possibility of such a condition and the tendency that it could be passed on from one generation to the next was not yet discovered, and Betty's ordinary mind could not work out such intricacies. All she could think of was, God had put a curse on her. "It's a curse, it's a curse," she hollered.

That night she sobbed and sobbed until she fell asleep.

The night nurse felt sorry for her so she did not wake her at the usual time of 6am the following morning. Exhausted, she slept and slept until 10am, then, rising slowly, she could hear faint noises around her. Through her dizzy eyes she could see six mothers all breast-feeding their babies – babies pulling, sucking, nibbling; mothers crooning, whispering, "Ga ga, ga ga," over them. It was such a moving spectacle; she could take it no more.

"Oh God, what have I... Nurse! Nurse! I want to see my baby. Bring her to me. Please, please, bring me baby to me," she screamed. And with that, Sadie, the little Jamaican nurse shot out of her seat and scurried away. Within minutes she returned with the little bundle in her arms.

"Here you are," Sadie said, "your little bag of tricks."

Betty held the baby tentatively at first, feeling her warmth; looking at her face; her body; she could see her slanting eyes; small head; her little mouth with her tongue just sticking out a little; slightly short arms and body unlike that of her other six children when they were born. This one was different: with its soft fair hair, it looked almost like a porcelain doll. She stared at it and slowly, slowly, the cold, numb feeling began to melt. Caught up in anguish too deep for tears, she could not even cry.

Slowly, she held the baby a little closer, squeezing her a little, then, all of a sudden she cooed, "my little bag of tricks… yes, that's it," she whispered, "I shall call her Trixie."

And so Trixie Avril O'Connor was born at 9am, October 17th 1945, to Betty and Tom O'Connor. 'A Librian girl, balance of the scales' – so they say and well!

She weighed just 7 lbs.

Betty's thoughts were working overtime now as she looked at her little porcelain-like baby. 'Useless,' they said, 'mentally retarded, Huh,' and, as she thought, she heard a cry coming from deep down inside her saying:

I give you this child, a gift to all of you…
Eternal innocence. To you she looks imperfect
but to me she looks flawless…She will evoke
the kindness that will keep you human…
She is a sign to you…Treasure her.

And so she, Betty O'Connor, had made up her mind. She, Betty, was going to give her child, Trixie, that chance. A chance to live a full life, come what may. She couldn't hold back the tears that were welling up inside of her and she began sobbing.

She nestled Trixie closer to her, pulled out her breast and put the nipple into Trixie's mouth.

Before long Trixie began sucking… slowly, slowly, she nibbled but something was wrong. Trixie was not sucking properly.

It took Betty nearly two hours to breast-feed Trixie and so she knew that something was not quite right.

CHAPTER THREE

Betty was back home and she was glad; glad but sad.

She stepped out of the taxi into 17 Millers End with some trepidation. Inside, the children were waiting to greet her and their newborn baby sister, Trixie. "Ba ba! Ba ba!" 2 year-old Joey stuttered.

"Y-es ba-by, pretty ba-be," 20 year-old Jennifer cooed.

They'd heard she wasn't normal but that didn't bother them. They were a strongly bonded Irish family and they would love and care for their little sister no matter what package she came in. Thick and thin, they would stick together, be there for her, or so they thought.

They had made a bed from hand-me-down blankets and sheets and laid it in the corner of the front room. That was to be Trixie's crib for a while to come.

No nursery, no funny, fancy paintings with pink nursery rhymes dotted here and there, and no little crib standing in the middle either – they were too poor for that. They didn't have enough money to buy food and keep warm, let alone a fancy nursery.

Jennifer took the baby from Betty's arm and laid it on the bed of rags. "Ga ga! Ga ga!" Jennifer said. The baby screamed.

That night Trixie hollered and hollered and Betty was up most of the night, changing nappies or breast-feeding her, but Trixie still couldn't suck properly. By morning, Betty was worn out, exhausted. Then, a few days later Trixie got diarrhoea – loose stools running everywhere it seemed. Betty was washing countless nappies made from old rags and now she was running out of places to hang them to dry.

She'd tried everything, from gripe water to salt water – all to no avail. Then someone told her to try sugar water. "No milk," they'd asserted. "Stick to the water and it would soon stop." So Betty tried it and miraculously the diarrhoea stopped.

A month later Trixie got an eye infection and then she got the chest infection. The doctor treated her with antibiotics, but he could do nothing about the damp house in which Trixie lived.

That was a social condition, or so he believed.

The room in which Trixie lived was cold. In fact the whole house was cold. Tom O'Connor wasn't working and they couldn't afford to buy coal to heat the house, so 15 year-old Michael used to go down to the woods nearby and collect dead wood – branches, chippings, anything, so long as it would light up and heat the house.

But Trixie's health continued to deteriorate. From diarrhoea to chest infections, from feeding problems to eye infections, she continued to suffer. The repeated visits to the doctor were beginning to tell on Betty's health too – but she soldiered on.

Then one evening, suddenly, she heard a choking, gurgling sound coming from Trixie's bed. Like a flash, Betty darted over. She could see the colour draining from Trixie's face, her lips turning white. "Quick, quick," she hollered at 17 year-old Edna, "Go get de doctor."

With fear in her eyes, Betty grabbed Trixie from the bed. Trixie's body went limp, placid, as if every muscle in her body was turning to jelly. Quickly, she laid her on her back, then blew into her mouth and pressed her ribcage. She blew and pressed, blew and pressed until Trixie's ribcage started to move. Trixie gasped and belched, then slowly the colour started trailing back to her face and Trixie O'Connor was breathing again.

Betty O'Connor had given Trixie the kiss of life and now she was alive again.

It took the doctor 15 minutes to arrive. But when he examined Trixie, he could find no cause for her 'blackout.' She was only six months old.

Every day Betty would be up at 5'o clock in the morning till 12'o clock at night, slaving away; washing; cleaning; cooking; shopping – it never stopped. But Betty loved her 7 children and hard as it was and poor as they were, she was determined to give them a good, loving, caring family life; a good Irish family upbringing – especially Trixie – she had to give this one every chance to live a decent life.

Regularly, she used to massage Trixie's body, moving her limbs rhythmically to the humming of Nursery rhymes; 'Pat-a-Cake, Pat-a-cake… This Little Piggy… etc.' She used to teach Trixie to grip her fingers then raise and lower her in time with the rhymes. Then one day they nailed a wooden pole in the corner of the front room and hung brightly coloured hand-me-down toys across Trixie's line of vision, so that she could reach up and grab them.

But, even though she was practising each manoeuvre at a time, Trixie was hardly making any progress. Being mentally retarded, her thought process was slow to grasp any teachings, especially if they were new. All she did was holler and holler and fell over each time Betty tried to sit her up.

Betty began to get despondent. "Will my child ever be able to do anything?" she cried to herself, but still she persevered. She knew she had to keep on trying, for her child's sake. She never gave up hope.

Then one day, when Trixie was one-years-old, she grasped and pulled some toys down from the wooden pole. She screamed and screamed as though she would crack the earth, and Betty was over the moon.

And so it went, on and on and on…

When she was 2 years old, she managed to pull herself up and sit on her bottom, clinging to her favourite rag doll as it hung from the pole above her. She cooed, "a-ah, a-a-h…"

It took Trixie 2 years to do this and Betty was almost jumping for joy. But with Trixie's continued bouts of chest infections and frequent visits to the doctor; visits here, clinic there, Betty's health was failing, especially since she had no support from her husband Tom, who continued to drown his sorrows in drink.

Tom O'Connor was an honest hard-working man. He had been in the Army during the Second World War and always sent home regular wages to keep his family. But a few months before Trixie's birth the Army discharged him – the war had ended and they didn't need gunners any more. They couldn't put him out on the streets though; what with 6 children to keep, they had to let him rent the Army's house in which his family lived, else they, the Army, would be disgraced. And so Tom O'Connor was now a jobless man.

With most of the industries having been bombed out and with no skills of his own except labouring, every day he trailed the streets of Titville looking for work: road digging, hod carrying, rubbish clearing, building, anything – so long as he could feed his children – but nothing came.

He went to a smithy's yard: No hands wanted. He went to a biscuit factory: No workers needed. He staggered into a builder's yard: No labourers wanted for hire.

Every day he dragged himself along the highways and byways, only to be told he wasn't needed. Sometimes he travelled for 10 miles, backwards and forwards he trudged, only to return home in despair, exhausted, worn out, a dead man.

One day, he waited for 12 hours at a builders yard, dust choking his lungs as he coughed and spluttered, hanging out in the cold, hoping he would hear his name called out, but it never happened. There simply was just no work for him. Tom O'Connor was a demoralised man – all but dead.

And so, lost in a world beyond redemption, he took to drinking. He had no money but the bartenders used to fill his glass up. "One more for de road, aye, eh Tom," they would say as they topped it up, free of charge. And so it went. On and on… the birth of their Mongol child Trixie, heightening his sense of despair. He was a demoralised man who couldn't take any more, so he drank himself stupid.

Every day he would trail the streets of Titvile looking for work and every evening he would return home with no work, pissed out of his mind. He had sunk to the abyss of despair. It was as if he could face life no more so he sought solace in booze.

On Social Security Income of 75shillings a week, out of which 13shillings was used to pay the rent and 12shillings for Trixie to attend the Child Centre, Betty was left with 50shillings a week with which to feed and clothe her children, heat the house and pay any other household bills. Not surprisingly, the children wore second-hand clothes and had few hand-me-down toys to play with, given to them by charities.

There was no money for entertainment either. She couldn't afford to take them on a bus ride, never mind a trip to the funfair. And there was no meat for their Sunday lunch too. Bacon pudding was all they had to contend with. Sometimes, Betty used to get so distressed, she would cry and cry, but still she laboured on. What else could she do? She loved her family so…

As usual, Tom would do his daily rounds returning home at night, stinking drunk. They never knew whether he looked for work or not. He never told anyone and Betty was past caring.

Then one day he stumbled home early, pissed out of his mind as usual. It was Thursday and Betty had just returned from shopping. Trixie was howling, screaming her head off – she had a chest infection and Betty was going out of her mind.

"Shut dat chile up," he drawled.

The baby's screams continued and Tom O'Connor was going mad.

"Shut dat idiot up! You hear me, Mrs O'Connor. Ah say, shut it up! A man got no peace in his own house. Every night ah come 'ome to dat ravin' lunatic. Shut it up, ah say. You hear me Mrs O'Connor, oh ah go shut it up meself!"

Betty O'Connor had had enough of this drunken husband and now she lost her bearings.

"Who are you to talk Tom O'Connor? Every night you come 'ome pissed out of you mine, leavin' me alone all day to fen for dem children: cookin', washin', cleanin'. You 'ave no right O'Connor... you 'ave no say in dis 'ouse."

Tom O'Connor couldn't take that. He went raving mad. He raised his fist to lash out at Betty, but he was so stoned, he circled, lost his balance and crashed onto the floor like a sack of potatoes, unconscious.

The distraught Betty left him lying there for the rest of the night, whilst she tended to her children and went to bed, late as usual.

She was so distressed, she shook with fear. She couldn't believe that Tom could ever attempt to hit her, but he did and all she could do was cry herself to sleep.

CHAPTER FOUR

Hugging the pain and anguish to herself, in her loneliness she had no one to turn to, nowhere to go. She couldn't even take the children out shopping. Their ragged appearance used to make people stop and stare. 'The only place left,' she thought, 'was the nearby woods where she could find some peace and quiet; a place where she could at least think,' she hoped.

So, the next day she got up early and took Darren, Joey and Trixie for a walk in the woods.

As they walked along, they could see dark steep hills in the far distance; wet misty land below tall mountains slumbering like lost giants in the midst. The children jumped and skipped about happily while bay windows from the nearby low rise flats protruded around them, as if they had some myth to tell.

They walked and walked until they reached the woods. They noticed a stream bending into a semi-circle; badgers shuffling about and rabbits scurrying in and out of burrows. Joey and Darren chased them – wood-chips crunching under their little ragged feet.

The two boys scampered about, their keen eyes following the trail of a few fishes floating in between the lilies of the stream. Betty, holding Trixie in her arms, noticed a bee as it dived into a flower, sucking up its nectar. High above, a gull flew, every now and then, darting down to try and catch a fish – a morsel for the day.

'What a sight,' Betty thought, as it took her mind away from her troubles – for a fleeting moment, at least.

They fed the ducks and watched the swans as they glided majestically on the still water, leaving a trail of sparkling ripples along the way.

Betty returned home that day, refreshed, ready to face life again, but she and Tom didn't speak to each other for months after. Tom O'Connor knew he had to do something about it, to break the ice, at least.

One day, he rumbled in through the front door, drunk as usual. He was singing, drolling really: "my old man de dusman, he wears a dustman cap... Mrs O'Connor? Mrs O'Connor? Where's me sugar plum? 'Ere! Look wha' a brin' fo' me little Pixie. Ah bit ofe meat fo' Sunday dinner, me little Sugar... (he belched)... plum!"

Betty rushed to the front entrance to find him swinging a dead rabbit in his hand – he'd caught it in the woods and brought it home for her to cook. She couldn't keep her face straight. Tom O'Connor was back to his old tricks and she burst out laughing.

That Sunday they had roast rabbit for lunch, instead of the usual boiled potatoes and bacon leftovers given to them by a neighbour or two. It was the first Sunday they ever had meat for lunch in a long, long time.

With peace now made, Betty continued training Trixie. In time, she would teach her to stand, crawl, walk and talk, but for now she had to teach her to crawl. She turned her onto her tummy, placed her favourite ragdoll near her but out of her reach, then moved each knee in turn, singing her favourite rhymes and keeping her properly balanced so that she could stretch up and reach it. But Trixie became so frustrated that all she did was cry and cry and every time she just failed.

Betty however, did not give up. She tried again and again, until at last, one day Trixie started to crawl. She was 3 years old and Betty was relieved.

Now it was time to teach her to stand. So she suspended some toys above Trixie's head and the only way she could get them was to reach up and grab them. She stretched and fell, stretched and fell for a long long time. Then one day when she was four, she suddenly stood up. It was like a miracle.

It was time now to teach her to walk and that wasn't going to be easy either, but a little bit of bribery soon helped. Two people held her hand, whilst the third, placed one of her feet in front of the other, moving her forward as they went along. She tried and tried; the children gave her hugs and kisses each time she tried.

On and on it went, and so with the help of her siblings, after a year of trying, Trixie made her first step.

Now, Trixie O'Connor could walk and Betty was relieved.

Trixie was now 5 years old, but still couldn't talk. With her tongue drooping from her mouth, all she could do was make noises and Betty would get quite distressed, but she was determined to get her talking.

She would take her up to the bedroom to help make the beds and would say, "One sheet,"

"A-a-h!" Trixie would reply.

"Two sheets."

"T-a-a-h!" Trixie would answer.

"Blue sheet."

"A-a-a-h!" Trixie would drool.

And so it went. On and on. For months Betty tried, but she could not get Trixie to speak. There was no Educational Psychologist, no Portage to help her in that era, so in the end, Betty had to console herself with the thought that Trixie may never be able to speak. But, by the noises she made and the signs and gestures she'd learnt, Trixie could make herself heard and understood.

During those times, Jennifer and Jimmy used to give Betty a few extra bob or two from the wages they earned at the laundry. But times were tough. With no wages coming from Tom and such little money, plus the constant pressure of looking after Trixie and no breaks at all, it began to affect Betty's health.

Betty O'Connor was getting thinner and thinner. Her abdomen was swelling and sometimes she felt sick too. She had lost so much weight that she decided she must go and see the doctor.

"Doctor, sometime de pain in me stomach is so bad, like a tornado inside me, rumbling and tumbling, burnin' me stomach out. An' sometime' ah feel so sick ah wan' to die."

"All right Mrs O'Connor," the doctor replied after listening in earnest. "But I think I'll have to send you for some tests." He sent her for x-rays and blood tests – this test, that test, so many tests. Then, at last the results came and he sent for her.

"Mrs O'Connor, I have news for you." He didn't look happy and Betty could tell. "Not so good, I am afraid…"

Betty was getting anxious but she tried to put on a brave face.

"Mrs O'Connor, I'm afraid you have a cyst, an ovarian cyst!" He said, "and they will have to operate on you when a bed becomes available."

He then went on to explain what the operation entailed while Betty listened with fear in her heart. Then, all of a sudden the distraught Betty cried out, "Oh no, oh no! Doctor and what about Trixie? Ah know de family would look after 'er, especially Jennifer and Edna – dey love 'er so. But she is only 5 and… you know doctor… retarded."

"Don't worry, Mrs O'Connor. Don't worry."

"But I am worried Doctor. We wan'er stay wit' 'er family. Dey love 'er so, so much, Doctor, so…"

"Don't worry, Mrs O'Connor," he cut in sharply. "I'll take care of everything. There's not a thing to worry about," he assured her. But Betty wasn't sure. With that puzzled look on the Doctor's face, her heart was thumping one to the dozen, as she made her way home that day.

He didn't waste time. Within minutes of her leaving the clinic, he was on the phone talking to the community nurse, discussing Betty's situation.

She, in turn, phoned the social visitor and a visit was promptly arranged.

The phones had buzzed and the wheels were now in motion.

Betty O'Connor wanted her family to stay together whilst she was in hospital. But no one heard her cry:

My journey stretches onward.
And as I take each step, it moves on and on…
No end in sight.
Oh, how it's risky!
But I know you are there somewhere,
Taking each step with me, as I take them…

They never did hear her cry. They, the professionals, had taken care of things. They had taken charge of her life and now the social visitor was to pay her a visit.

CHAPTER FIVE

Pamela Hickson cycled down Millers End with some reservation. Ahead, rows of red brick terraced houses lined the streets on either side, their chimneys shooting out like muzzles of hot guns, lying in wait, ready to fire at the first line of enemies. All but one was smokeless.

It was early June 1950 and with the war long over, most of the inhabitants of these Army houses had since moved on, leaving the houses empty – their windows crackling to the wild wind, every now and then.

Somewhere in the distance a lone dog howled – a long mournful note, a menacing noise, followed by a series of loud barks, as Pamela Hickson approached nearer. Like the Hound of Baskerville, it mourned, crying, as if laying in wait to spring on its prey.

Pamela Hickson felt on edge and very uneasy.

Inside No 17, Betty O'Connor waited anxiously for the woman she thought was going to help her. She had done everything. She'd cleaned the house, tidied up here and there. She'd even lit the fire so that the smell of the damp, cold musty air would disappear. And in her excitement, she decided to lay the table with her special teapot, cups and saucers and set them on the wooden table against the chairs that Tom O'Connor had built for them.

Then she heard the knock on the door.

"Come in Miss…" Betty invited, as she opened the door.

"Miss Hickson!" Pamela asserted as she entered, her beady eyes snapping up every shadow; every crack; trace of dust; food droppings; dirty clothing; anything she could see along that hallway – like a camera, she took it all in.

"Would you like a cup of tea?" Betty enquired, courteously, pulling out a chair for Pamela to sit on.

"Yes, splendid, splendid!" Pamela retorted, not shifting her gaze for a split second from the surroundings her mind's eye was now recording.

To save time, Betty had previously boiled the kettle on the open fire, so that it only took a minute or so for it to heat up.

"Milk? Sugar?"

"Yes. Yes, two sugars. Sweet tooth, you know – sweet tooth."

Betty poured the tea, placed two teaspoonfuls of sugar in the cup and then added milk from the little she had left over to feed her own family. She was about to hand it to Pamela when she noticed Pamela wiping the chair briskly with her handkerchief. Pamela then sat gingerly on it. She held the cup, sniffed, and then began sipping slowly, her lips barely touching it. It was as if she might catch some unknown disease.

Poor Betty, she looked on in awe.

Pamela barely took a sip or two, when she put the cup down and began firing questions.

"And now, Mrs O'Connor, Trixie's full name? Date of birth? How many children in the family? Seven?... yes, seven," Pamela continued, screwing up her nose at each question. "Family's income...! Yes, Yes..." she was so patronising.

"Thump!" little Trixie threw a rag doll across the floor and Pamela Hickson jumped.

"We were saying... Family income... Yes... 75shillings a week."

Rent...............e-mmh!... 13 shillings a week.

Child care..............12 shillings a week."

'E-mmh' Pamela thought again. 'That leaves Betty 50shillings with which to buy food, clothe her children and generally live on. E-mmh!.

She probed and delved, delved and probed, every now and then pulling her chair back away from Betty, as if a flea would jump from Betty's clothes and land on her. Betty was getting quite distressed.

"Thump!" Trixie tossed another toy across the floor.

Betty got up and gave Trixie her favourite blue rag doll, but Pamela Hickson sat there as if glued to the chair. She searched and probed, searched and probed again, until she'd exhausted all the options. All but one question was left – that would come later.

But Betty's mind was working overtime, her head was spinning. "50shillings a week to live on. Miss Hickson," Betty appealed, "Ah 'ave to pay 12shilling a week to take Trixie to de Child Welfare Centre, two times a week; dat leave me wit' notin' much to feed me family, heat de 'ouse. Ah really car'n afford it, Miss Hickson."

Pamela Hickson already knew that. Her calculating mind had long since fathomed it out. But she paid no attention to Betty's cry. Instead, she carried on unceremoniously, putting on a stiff front, as the coal fire blazed away in front of her.

"Miss Hickson!..." 'Crack!'... A small speck of burnt out wood shot out of the fire sending a shower of flames. Like a tongue of fire it glided upwards, then, 'bang!' it landed straight on Miss Hickson's frame, dead! Startled, she frisked it away quickly, and like lightening, it was gone as quickly as it came.

"Miss Hickson?... More?..."

Pamela Hickson was getting mad. She rambled on and on... until the distraught Betty could take no more. She'd had enough. She didn't want to hear another word.

She thought Miss Hickson had come to help her and now this woman... spewing all this garbage at her, 'she didn't mention the fat salary she was earning, this Miss... what do you call her?... The money she used, to buy the beautiful necklace she was wearing; the expensive perfume, which lingered as she whisked past; the specially-made clothes, so well pressed – Betty could almost smell the starch as Pamela

Hickson went past – Whilst she, Betty and her family, lived on cast off clothing and bacon leftovers for lunch.'

Busy, jotting down notes until she had all the answers but one, Pamela Hickson continued searching, probing, searching, every now and then glancing around, as if that flea or worst still the mites might attack her and savage her body to pieces.

"Oh!… and Oh!… one last question Mrs O'…

"Yes?…"

Your husband Tom has not been able to find much work since they discharged him from the Army 5 years ago?"

"And?…" The tearful Betty looked at her with pain in her eyes.

"Is it true he comes home drunk every night?" Pamela quizzed. "Has he ever beaten or abused you or the children?"

Betty was so shocked, it was as if a bolt of lightening had just struck her down. She wasn't sure whether she should answer this question or not, but she wasn't sophisticated enough to avoid it. She would do anything to keep her family together, so she answered the questions honestly and straight-forwardly, hoping that would be the end of the matter.

Poor Betty. She just didn't understand the game.

She told Miss Hickson everything; how Tom used to come home drunk; how he would argue; how one day he tried to hit her. On she went, Miss Hickson scribbling each note with the eye of a hawk, her face mapping out the scene like an automatic movie camera.

With precision, she took it in: the bed of rags in the corner where Trixie laid; the dust on the worn-out rug that the broom could not suck up; the food droppings on the kitchen floor; the damp musty smell of the house. Her beady eyes took it all in as she scribbled on.

"And now Mrs O'Connor, I would like to see the children's bedrooms?"

Four boys, age 23 to 7, sleeping in one room; two girls, age 20 and 17, sleeping in the other; Betty, Tom and 5 year old Trixie sleeping in the third. No furniture, just beds with hand-me-down blankets and sheets; worm-eaten boxes in which they stored their clothes; a mirror standing in the hallway, so pitiful it would break anyone's heart.

But Pamela Hickson continued on her mission, unperturbed. Like a sponge, she was sapping it all in.

From room to room she walked apprehensively, noting the damp patches on the walls and the flakes from the ceiling ready to fall. Then, a sickly feeling took hold of her: 'that flea again,' she thought, 'or was it a mouse, lying at bay, ready to spring on her at a moment's notice?'

She was jumpy now. Then, all of a sudden she turned round. "Mrs O'Connor, in a few weeks time you will be going into hospital to have your operation. There is no-one capable of looking after Trixie here.

Betty looked at her with fear in her eyes.

"Your elder kids go out to work and your husband is inebriated most of the time."

Betty's heart sank.

"Your younger kids are not capable of looking after her."

Betty began to shiver.

"Trixie is, after all a 5 year old Mongol."

Betty could feel her temperature rising.

"And… Mrs O'Connor, there are many capable well-to-do families out there, from Mrs Peabody's Organisation, who are crying out to give Trixie a comfortable home."

Betty's heart missed a beat.

"One in particular I have in mind, is Mrs Gwendoline Hanrahan. She is a kind and caring lady and she would give Trixie a wonderful home."

Betty's heart thumped wildly.

"It would only be temporary, until you return from hospital…"

The words pierced like a dagger in Betty's mind. A cold shadow enveloped her body, her face, her mind, her everything. She felt sick… She felt dizzy… She didn't hear anymore.

"Are you alright, Mrs O'Connor?"

"Yes… yes…" she stuttered, waking from the daze, the fright Miss Hickson had just given her.

"Trixie will be looked after well, I promise you."

"Yes… yes…Betty replied, shocked, as if a mighty thunderbolt had just struck her and the life had sprung out of her body.

"Just a few formalities you know, a few papers to sign, that's all."

"I shall arrange it and let you know," Miss Hickson continued. "You must think of your health, you know," she added, as she made her way to the front door.

'Yes, yes,' Betty was thinking, her mind wheeling, leaping in bounds, like the waves of a stormy sea. Thoughts whizzing about in her head, as she led Pamela Hickson to the front door.

'De gall of da' woman,' she was thinking. 'Ow could she come into me 'ouse, enjoy me 'ospitality, den spy on me. Spy! De tin-faced, ugly, beaky-nosed bitch! 'Ow could she know 'ow it feel like, she doesn't 'ave no kids of 'er own.'

'Ah bet she was adopted, salvaged from some poor family and determine' to show de world 'ow to put it right,' climbe' de social ladder by any means she could. Spy on de poor, destroy dem if she has to.'

Betty's mind was reaching crescendo now and she was about to boil over.

'An' ah bet dere are 'oles in 'er curtain too, she 'avent washed dem for years; mites in 'er chair; scrap in 'er kitchen floor 'cause she was too lazy to clean it; and damp on de wall of 'er rented flat.'

'But no one 'ould ever know dat, would dey? No big boy wachin' 'er, ready to sprin dere 'orse dung on 'er face, as she did me. Yes, dats de way it is. She is a Social Visitor an 'er word is Gods word.'

Until now, Betty had no idea how the social work system operated. Now, she was getting the message hard and fast and she just didn't know how to handle it.

36

'Ah shown de children how to look after Trixie an dey did a lot to 'elp me,' her mind was torturing her. 'Dey would care for Trixie, dey promise. Dey wouldn't want us to split up. Dey woul' do anytin to keep de family togeder…'

"Are you alright, Mrs O'Connor?" Miss Hickson intercepted her thoughts, as she reached out to open the front door.

"Yes, Yes… Ok … Ok!" Betty replied, shaking like a volcano ready to erupt.

'Bitch! Devious bitch! Wicked bitch! Spy! Evil spy! Bitch!'

Betty was just about to scream out, but somehow she couldn't. Instead… bang! She slammed the front door shut, so hard that Miss Hickson nearly tripped and fell over the steps.

Oh! How she would have loved to punch that Pamela Hickson on the nose.

Hugging the pain all to herself, she rushed to the front room, sat on the chair and sobbed her heart out with Trixie hollering beside her.

Betty O'Connor was too poor, too sick. She didn't have the muscle or the money to fight Miss Hickson or the system. And there was no Downs Syndrome Association, no MENCAP to fight it for her at the time – they simply did not exist.

Betty O'Connor was all done in. Her spirits crushed – broken.

CHAPTER SIX

Eccentric millionairess Jane Peabody, was a Londoner who devoted her life to improving the care and welfare of mentally retarded people, especially children.

Born in the late 19th century, she witnessed first hand, the appalling conditions of mental institutions in England; conditions in which these children lived and suffered.

In despair she watched as, day after day, week after week, they sat together: weak and able-bodied, feeble and strong-minded, lunatics and near normal, young and old – there they were, strung together in cold, cramped, claustrophobic rooms, or huddled along plain-walled corridors, like prisoners in cells waiting to be heard.

Week by week, she watched on her visits. Some wailing like lone wolves, others shouting, crying out. "Help! Help! Miss… Help!" some spitting, some urinating on the floor. She heard a woman howling, "Me baby! Me baby" Miss, Miss… she take me baby…"

Day after day, she watched children huddled together in the corners of cold icy rooms, crawling, staring at blank walls or simply screaming; nothing to do but watch – no stimulation, no training – such luxuries unheard of until the 1970s and 80s, when the Education Act swiftly brought them into force.

They were staring, these siblings, vacant expressions on their faces; able-bodied adults cleaning, scrubbing floors, helping with petty tasks or simply marching up and down the corridors, calling out to any passer by.

One day, Miss Peabody saw a little Mongol girl crawling on all fours, picking up scraps of food from the floor, faeces;

urine, leaking from her half-naked body – the staff too busy, too rushed off their feet to tend to her.

It was too much for her. She, Miss Peabody couldn't take any more, so she decided to do something. 'Anything was better than nothing,' she thought.

'These children must be moved from such brutal, heart-rending environments,' the distraught Miss Peabody thought to herself. 'Moved to live with families who would give them a normal family life; love them; support them; for without such love they merely exist.' And so the determined Jane set about her task.

She badgered and pressured, charmed and beguiled every politician, each and any person in power she came across. She signed petitions, recruited people to support her, until finally in 1899 her dreams came true. She was able to start a scheme for families in Brightonstone, to take in mentally handicapped people from London, for holidays or short-term stay.

'At last she was able to do something about these suffering people,' she thought. But little did she know that she was on the start of something big. Things really began to move.

In 1914, the Guardianship Society was formed, then in 1920 its First Constitution and Principles of Care was drafted in line with the Mental Deficiency Act 1913. And so the Peabody Organisation was born: a humane society founded to give mentally handicapped people a better quality of life; an improvement on the lifestyle they were living; a chance to live a fuller life.

But like all charities, her Organisation was soon caught up in mayhem. It had to conform to bureaucratic red tape: laws; rulings; documents; forms; a hodge-pot of papers to be filled in and signed, before a child could be placed in its care. At least eight papers had to be signed: Applications Forms; Social Visitors Report; Parent's Consent; Medical Certificates signed by two doctors; Petition for an Order; Declaration by two people; Statement of Particulars and finally The Order itself sending the mentally retarded child into Miss Peabody's guardianship and care.

The list could have gone on and on, but some bright spark decided enough was enough and went on to put a spanner in its works.

Ironic, isn't it? All Miss Peabody wanted was to provide family homes for these children, but now her Organisation was sucked into the very ghost she tried to avoid – the bureaucratic vending machine, a bureaucratic milieu – papers! Papers! And more papers! All filed away in some strong-armed cabinet, waiting to be fished out and signed!…signed!… signed!

CHAPTER SEVEN

Weak from a hangover after days on the booze, Tom O'Connor arrived at 10am sharp, Thursday morning, at Miss Hickson's office. He could barely carry himself.

He knocked on the door.

"Come in! Come in! Mr O'Connor. Sit! Sit! Do sit down!" Miss Hickson commanded, pulling a chair out and placing it as far away as possible, from her.

It was a move she made, not only because she feared that a flea might jump from Mr O'Connor's clothes and suck out her very soul, but also because she wanted to keep a safe distance from the stench that was coming from them. He stank to high heaven.

She knew that he was quite inebriated and she could see from the drawn-out sallow look on his face, that he was a worried man too, but she continued to delve in her stiff and starchy manner.

"And how are you Mr O'Connor?" she probed, "keeping well I hope?"

"Jus' keeping dem wolves alive," he drolled, not caring a hoot about her attitude or her questions.

"Good to hear that. Good! Good!" she intercepted, bluntly.

He didn't answer.

"And how is Mrs O'Connor?" she continued in her busy manner.

"Bearing up me lady. Bearin' up, your Honour," he grunted, shuffling in his chair. But Miss Hickson took no notice of his sarcasm.

"And little Trixie?" she continued probing. Tom O'Connor did not reply.

With a sick wife going into hospital and now this half-witted child about to go into care, all he wanted was to sign the papers quickly, get it over and done with as fast as he could and go back to the pub and drown his sorrows.

Tom O'Connor was a battered man spiralling down to a place of no return, but no one noticed.

"Pamela Hickson didn't like the man, but she tried to break the ice as coolly as an ice maiden. He didn't like her either, so before long she got the hint and tried to get on with the job the only way she knew how.

"And now Mr O'Connor," she insisted, "here is the Form of Consent, which I would like you to sign."

She pushed the paper swiftly under his nose and said, "Sign here please, sign here," she indicated, pointing to a spot marked signature.

By now, Tom O'Connor was welling up inside, but he chose to ignore her blunt behaviour. He could not read or write and so could not understand what the paper said, but would sign a blank piece of paper if he had to, in order to get Trixie looked after.

Then, all of a sudden, his brain came alive. Like a furnace on fire, it burned and crackled in his head. He was sweating. He was shaking and he was ready to sign that form, a form headed:

Form of Consent by Parent (Mental Deficiency Act 1913 – 1938).
It read:

I, the undersigned (Tom O'Connor) being the parent of Trixie Avril O'Connor, who is alleged to be a defective within the meaning of the above Acts, do hereby consent to a petition being presented to a judicial authority for an Order under the provisions of the said Acts, in respect of the said Trixie O'Connor.

Dated this 27th day of June 1950
17 Millers End, Titville.

Tom O'Connor could not write, so with sweat pouring from his face and hands trembling like a frightened rabbit, he signed on the spot where Miss Hickson had pointed. And so the deed was done.

He didn't understand a word of it, but that didn't matter. What mattered was, he couldn't cook, he couldn't wash, he could hardly look after himself and he was a drunk. So how could he look after his 5 year old retarded daughter, Trixie? He was stumped.

He knew he couldn't care for his little Trixie so he gave his consent for her to be cared for. He thought it was only going to be for a while, at least whilst Betty was in hospital. What he didn't understand was that it was a move to take Trixie, their little retarded girl away from them for good.

He thought he was putting his name to a piece of paper in order to get Trixie cared for, for a while only.

Poor Tom, he just didn't understand the workings of the Social Care system.

Pamela Hickson had pulled the threads and Tom and Betty O'Connor were neatly stitched in.

CHAPTER EIGHT

It didn't take long for Pamela Hickson to get moving and before long she had it all fixed.

She picked up the phone… "Mrs Hanrahan?"

"Yes, it's she."

"Mrs Hanrahan? Pamela Hickson here."

"Yes Miss Hickson?"

"I've found her. I've found her Mrs Hanrahan. The perfect child for you."

"You've found her, oh my!" (Mrs Hanrahan was beside herself).

"Yes Mrs Hanrahan, I've found her. A beautiful little Mongol girl called Trixie. She is 5 years old and she is adorable!"

In fact, when Pamela visited Betty she did not find Trixie adorable at all. She found her quite threatening, frightening really and so she had kept her distance – didn't even speak to the child once. And now… all this…?

"She is adorable, Mrs Hanrahan! Did you hear that? She is simply a…"

Excited, Mrs Hanrahan couldn't wait to hear more.

"And!… Mrs Hanrahan," Pamela continued, "I will be bringing her down on Friday morning. Her father came last week and signed his consent and you'll have her. Temporarily, of course – that is… till all the papers are signed. Then, Mrs Hanrahan! You can have Trixie for as long as you wish."

Vi Hanrahan didn't understand the intricacies of Pamela Hickson's conversation – what was going on behind the scene. Pamela Hickson didn't tell her why Trixie was being placed temporarily in her care.

She didn't say that Trixie was being moved from the O'Connor's (a place of danger) to the Hanrahan's (a place of safety). Mrs Hanrahan didn't know that. All she cared about now, was getting the child she'd long waited for and she was over the moon.

Betty too wasn't told what was happening behind the scenes. Betty O'Connor loved her family dearly. She'd cared for them endlessly, sometimes putting her own life at risk. They were poor, sure; lived in a dilapidated house, sure; but she'd given them all the love and care she could muster. Tom was a drunkard, sure; but he loved his children dearly, never ill-treated them once. Couldn't she, Miss Hickson see that?

But Betty O'Connor didn't know what Miss Hickson was filing. It was just as well, for even if she knew she was too powerless to fight Pamela, the big woman; too muscle-less to fight that great big mighty powerhouse – the thing they called the Social System. That was top secret information, devised by Pamela, confidentially recorded, tucked away safely in her big brown file, locked away in that bureaucratic hothouse and only they knew what was in it.

Unaware of the dilemma she was letting herself in for, Mrs Hanrahan's heart was brimming with joy.

Ever since she'd lost her Jack she had sunk into a sea of despair. In her loneliness, she had wept and wept, cried so much until somebody told her about Miss Peabody's Organisation. 'There, she'd be able to find a child to love, to keep her company,' they told her. And so she set about getting a child.

Now at last, they'd found her one. A little mentally retarded girl called Trixie and Mrs Hanrahan was a happy woman.

Oh! How she was happy!

CHAPTER NINE

Outside 37 Vicars Lane, Mrs Hanrahan waited anxiously. She had seen the Peabody van racing down the road and had come outside to meet Miss Hickson and the child, Trixie. She was standing there watching and waiting when; all of a sudden it swerved round the bend and stopped. The driver then dropped them off and departed as quickly as he came.

"Good morning! Mrs Hanrahan," Miss Hickson greeted. She wasn't sure how Mrs Hanrahan would take to the child, but now, there she was waiting, and Miss Hickson was relieved. "I hope you haven't been waiting too long in the cold," she added.

"Not at all, not at all!" Mrs Hanrahan cut in, trying to be polite, the chill wind biting into her loosely-clad body."

"Here is the little girl you have been waiting for, little Trixie O'Connor. Isn't she sweet?…"

Taken aback by what she saw, Mrs Hanrahan went a little weak at the knees, but quickly pulled herself together, muscled her courage and stretched out her hand to greet Trixie.

Piercing blue eyes in a cherub-like face met her gaze; blonde curls bobbing up and down; and a tongue protruding in and out of a small mouth as if in tune with the chill wind.

Mrs Hanrahan was so shocked, but she tried to put on a brave front and offer a warm welcome to the little girl. "Hello Trixie," she went, stretching out both hands to hold Trixie's. But the child just stood there, staring.

Having lost her own child, Berty, and her husband, having been taken barely a year ago, she was indeed a very lonely woman, desperate for someone to fill the gap and so she was grateful that at last they'd found her a little girl to keep her company. 'Mongol or not,' she thought, 'I will do all I can to give this child a loving caring home and try to make her as happy as did my own family.'

She had made up her mind. She was going to care for the child, come what may. So, her voice barely audible, she declared, "Come on! Let's go in," and with that she pushed the door open and led them straight into her sumptuous front parlour.

"Cup of tea, Miss Hickson?"

"No, No!" Miss Hickson replied. "I have to go. I have several people to see today and I must dash. Thank you! And with that she made her way swiftly to the front door and was gone as quickly as she entered, leaving the bewildered Mrs Hanrahan all alone to cope with the child.

Looking down at the little girl who earlier had given her such a fright, she said, "And you, Miss little surprise, a cup of milk for you, my dear? I'm going to make you a strong little girl, you know." Then she filled a two-handled mug with milk and gave it to Trixie. But Trixie started to cry. She just wouldn't drink.

"Come on my little one, do try and drink your milk. It will make you strong, young lady, you know," she coaxed, but it landed on deaf ears. Trixie just sat there and cried. "Na-a-h, N-aa-h! Na-ah, Naa-h!" she howled, shaking her head as Betty had taught her to.

Mrs Hanrahan could not get through to Trixie, so she decided to go away for a few minutes in the hope that Trixie would calm down, but Trixie just sat there bawling her head off.

After a few minutes, Mrs Hanrahan returned. "Come on sweetie," she tried again, placing the cup into Trixie's mouth and attempting to feed her.

She could see that Trixie was hungry, so on and on, she coaxed... slowly, slowly... she coaxed and fed, coaxed and fed, until the cup was half-empty, most of it trickling down Trixie's neck, though.

Trixie had a feeding problem and so she was a slow drinker, but Mrs Hanrahan didn't know that, she just didn't understand. So she tried to feed her as she did her own children, only to watch Trixie getting more and more distressed.

That night Trixie got diarrhoea and Mrs Hanrahan hardly slept a wink. She was up half the night, changing and feeding her and trying to soothe her pain, but to no avail.

Trixie had a weak stomach – it was part of her condition and milk was the last feed anyone should have given her, but Mrs Hanrahan just didn't know that.

Every night, she would be up at least 3 times, changing Trixie's wet nappies (though Trixie was 5 years old she was still wetting herself) – and every morning, she was up at 5.30am, hollering and disrupting the place.

Trixie missed her family. She cried for them, pined for them, but since she couldn't speak, Mrs Hanrahan just didn't understand – In her own way, she tried and tried, did her best, but nothing worked. She wasn't getting much sleep and she was exhausted.

Every morning she'd be up at 5.30am, feeding Trixie with porridge or other soft foods, but Trixie wouldn't eat properly. She still had to be fed.

Mrs Hanrahan just did not understand. She simply put it down to temper tantrums. She'd seen too much of that with her own children and that's how she saw Trixie.

Gone five and half now, Trixie was still wearing nappies and it was beginning to get Mrs Hanrahan down. Day and night, Trixie would wet herself, soil herself; the brown telltale signs showing on her trousers. Mrs Hanrahan washed countless nappies and ran out of places to dry them. But still she kept on trying.

Over and over, she would show Trixie how to use the toilet, but often she forgot. Then, miraculously… Boom! She had used the toilet successfully and she was dry for 4 hours. Mrs Hanrahan was over the moon, "Dry, Dry!" she went, almost jumping with happiness.

"A-ah! A-a-ah!" Trixie nodded, chuckling away with joy. But come the next day, she was wet again. Poor mite, she just couldn't remember things for long. Her retarded mind just couldn't keep it there for long periods.

One day, she pulled out the toilet roll and blocked the toilet with it. Mrs Hanrahan had to call the plumber and she was fuming. Another time she tore up the toilet roll and scattered it all over Mrs Hanrahan's polished floor. Mrs Hanrahan went mad.

One sunny day, she took Trixie to visit some friends. Whilst they were eating, Trixie climbed up to the bathroom cupboard and plastered her face with haemorrhoid cream. The embarrassed Mrs Hanrahan, face red as a beetroot, had to leave her meal halfway and rush over to her rescue.

"Look what you've done, you silly girl," she shouted, "you could have harmed yourself," her hosts looking on bewildered. She washed and changed Trixie briskly and distraught, she departed home as quickly as her legs could carry her, leaving the unfinished, tasty meal behind her.

If she took Trixie to the park, Trixie would either strip herself naked, or sit on the damp ground hollering; at times, screaming herself to such a pitch, that Mrs Hanrahan would have to carry her home, briskly. And if she went out to the garden to get a breath of fresh air, she would return to find the contents of her kitchen cabinet strewn all over the floor, or her box of tissue torn up and strewn all over the place.

Day in, day out, Mrs Hanrahan struggled. No respite. No break. No special schools, no training places where Trixie could attend; nowhere to get extra help. Portage and other movements were unheard of in those days – and not until the 1970's and 1980's did they come into being. So all Mrs Hanrahan could do was soldier on.

One day, she sat Trixie on a chair and making gestures and pronouncing her words slowly, she quizzed, "Trixie, why do you tear up tissues and scatter them all over the place?" But Trixie didn't understand. All she did was shake her head

49

from side to side and holler. "N-ah, Na-ah! Na-ah, Na-ah!" she went, and Mrs Hanrahan had to give up.

Even though she was 6 years old now, she had a mental age of 3, but Mrs Hanrahan did not understand – poor soul! There were no psychology tests to guide her and no appropriate books either. And Langdon Downs, the man who discovered the symptoms of Mongolism, had more or less written it off as a hopeless case. He merely gave his name to it and called it Downs Syndrome.

It seemed she was all alone, doing the best she humanely could under the circumstances. But now she was coming to the end of her tether and there was no-one to help.

One day, when she was out in the garden, Trixie urinated on the kitchen floor, pulled out the kitchen drawers and Bang! Mrs Hanrahan's newly polished cutlery crashed straight onto the foul wet floor.

Hearing the crash, Mrs Hanrahan rushed into the kitchen. "Oh my god! What have you done?" she screamed, as she saw her silver cutlery lying there, seeping in urine. That was the last straw!

She could take no more and even though she cared for Trixie and wanted a little girl to love and cherish, like one of her own, she could not suffer any more torture. 'She'd had her for a year now,' she decided, 'and the time had come to send her packing.' So she stormed into the parlour, picked up the phone and dialled...

"Miss Hickson?"

"Yes, Miss Hickson here,"

"I've had enough! I've had enough, Miss Hickson. I cannot look after Trixie any more! I've..."

The distraught Mrs Hanrahan continued reeling off her turmoil down the phone, telling Miss Hickson all about Trixie's behaviour; her tricks; tantrums; trials; tribulations; Miss Hickson trying hopelessly to pacify her and persuade her, but to no avail.

She knew much about Trixie's unsavoury behaviour – it was there, recorded in her big brown file. And she knew too, that Mrs Hanrahan was a kind and caring lady and if she said she'd had enough, there was no point in pushing any further. So she badgered no more.

"Alright Mrs Hanrahan! OK, OK," calm down!" she pleaded. "No problem! We have another lady on the books you know, rearing to take Trixie in, so I'll be down tomorrow morning to take her to her new home."

And so now, at the age of six, Trixie was going to a new guardian. A hooked-nose spinster called Mildred Horseface from 11 Drivers Way, Brightonstone.

She was the best Miss Hickson could find.

CHAPTER TEN

Mildred's nose started to twitch. Her nose always twitched when she saw something she didn't like and she didn't like Trixie.

The child was cute enough, sure. With blonde curls dangling around a short stubby nose, she looked amusing really. But that tongue! Bobbing in and out of her mouth, quite frightening, it was; reminded her of something – yes, it reminded her of... that dream she used to have... about vampires descending on her soul and sucking the life out of her body. She felt queer; a little funny inside and she didn't like that. She began to sweat.

Ever since her sister Millie died two years ago, she'd lived a lonely life. A recluse really. Then the Peabody Organisation heard about her plight and promised to send her a little girl to keep her company. And now here she was. This... this alien creature from God knows where. Still, she wanted a little girl to care for – bring some life back into her dying soul. So she looked at the child, shook her head a little and promised she would care for her. Give it her best shot. Try the best she could no matter what. But it wasn't going to be easy.

Sometimes, Trixie would refuse to feed herself, especially if something upset her. She would get into a temper tantrum, refuse to eat or simply sit there with a vacant look on her face. But that didn't bother Mildred too much. Feeding Trixie was a chore she enjoyed, even though Trixie used to swing her head from side-to-side and half the food would trickle down the side of her neck. But it didn't bother Mildred too much.

Wetting the bed by night and soiling herself during the day, meant that two or three times a night Mildred would drag herself up, change Trixie's nappies and tend to her, washing countless nappies whilst not having much space left to hang them to dry.

She tried and tried to toilet train her but without much luck.

Then one day she went mad. She sat Trixie on the toilet and held her down. "Come on. Do it! Do it!" she shouted. Trixie howled and screamed. "Shut up. Do it! Do it!" she snapped. "Push! Push. Push it out!" she screamed, her eyes burning with fire.

Scared out of her wits, the child bawled and pushed, howled and pushed until both urine and faeces shot out of her shivering body like gunpowder from a charged gun.

"Good, now you can go and sit on your chair, she commanded, her angry face about to erupt, her nose twitching, twitching!

On another occasion, Mildred went to the shop next door to get some milk. When she returned her bathroom floor was covered with urine. Trixie had tried to use the toilet but missed it and wet the floor instead. Mildred's nose started to twitch again.

"Look what you've done, you dirty little girl! Come here, you horrid little girl."

She stormed towards Trixie, grabbed her by the neck, pushed her to the toilet then rushed to the kitchen, picked up the mop and shoved it towards Trixie's face. "Now you can mop it up. Mop! Mop!" she commanded, holding Trixie's hand round the mop, pushing and shoving, pushing and shoving, until the floor was almost dry. "That will teach you, you little monster. Don't you ever do that again!" She strapped Trixie onto the chair and went to the adjoining room to ponder.

Trixie sat there and cried her eyes out. Her retarded mind could not fathom out why she was being punished. 'She'd tried to use the toilet and now...?' She sobbed and sobbed until she fell asleep.

When Mildred decided to become Trixie's guardian, prepared to care for her, she read the literature sent to her from a hotchpotch organisation that had started in the 1950s, telling her about Downs Syndrome.

Reward, she regarded as nonsense. Punishment, she felt, was the key. 'A child could only learn what's right from wrong, by punishment,' she thought. So she set about to practise what she'd read and believed. She, Mildred, simply did not understand how to care for a little Mongol child.

Time went by and after a week or two Trixie was up to mischief again. It was Wednesday this time, when Mildred was greeted with another shock. Trixie had torn up her toilet tissues and spread them along the top of her polished mahogany dining table. Poor Trixie! She thought they were napkins.

She'd seen Mildred placing napkins on her table and tried to emulate her. Chuckling away, she was sure she had done something good, something that would really please Mildred. 'At last, at last!' her retarded mind was thinking. But Mildred didn't see it that way. She went mad.

"Not again!" she hollered. "Demented! Demented!" I've had enough! Had enough!" she snapped. She grabbed Trixie by the waist, lifted her off the floor and tried to strap her onto the chair, but Trixie just kept on screaming. "Na-ah, N-aah! Na-ah, N-aah!" she howled, swinging her head from side-to-side, kicking, dribbling, and hollering.

Losing her temper, Mildred slapped her hard on the face, and then quickly strapped her down. "You can stay there for an hour," she commanded, her face bright red. Fierce as a lion she was, as if about to strangle her prey. But she didn't. Instead, she went into the kitchen and cried her eyes out.

Week after week, month by month, the child, Trixie, endured torture and suffering, from this hook-nosed spinster, Mildred Horseface. A woman who never had a child of her own – a woman who didn't know how to bring up a normal child, let alone a Mongol one. But she tried. In her own way, how she did try. Punishment! Punishment! That was her weapon. And that tongue, lolling out of that child's mouth; it gave her the creeps.

Again and again, it sent her nose twitching but the Social Visitor never came. Pamela Hickson only ever visited once and then seemed to abandon them, forever.

On her own, Mildred persevered, but then one day the final straw came.

It was a warm spring day. The sun was shining. Like showers, it flickered its yellow-patterned beams onto Mildred's front windows and Mildred decided to do some gardening. Moulding, feeding, clipping and pruning, she tended her daffodils, singing away to herself. She was as happy as a lark. Then suddenly – bang! She heard a thud!

She rushed through to the kitchen to investigate the noise and was horrified by what she saw. There she was, little Trixie, sitting on the urinated floor, chuckling away to herself, mopping away with Mildred's newly-pressed kitchen towels.

"How dare you! You horror!" she screamed, her nose twitching. "Using my clean kitchen towels to mop that smelly floor. You horror! Horror! I've had enough! I've had enough!"

She pulled Trixie up by the hair, shoved the mop and bucket in her hands and pushed her out onto the front steps. "Mop! Mop! You monster!" she commanded, putting her hand round Trixie's and moving the mop backwards and forwards, backwards and forwards. Over and over, she went with the mop then, all of a sudden she left Trixie alone, to mop the front steps.

Tears were streaming down the child's face as she mopped and mopped for a solid hour. Inwards and outwards it went, the same movement, the same position. The stone steps grated under her unsuitably-clad feet as her body shivered from the cold, blustery winds. Poor child! She had no-one to turn to. No-one to listen.

In the distance, on they walked. Passers-by. Not taking a blind bit of notice. They thought the child was playing a game of mopping steps so they didn't bother to probe.

One man did stop. He stared, shrugged his shoulders, and then walked away again. Poor fellow! He just didn't understand.

If only she could speak she would have beckoned, called out to the man and say – "Sir, please, would you help me?" But she couldn't. She was dumb. Mentally retarded and he didn't even notice the little girl with the blonde curls sobbing her heart out.

He just walked on by.

Mildred Horseface wanted a child badly, but she didn't bargain for what she'd got. She'd reached the point of no return and now she could take no more. "That's it," she said. "I've had enough!" Burning with anger, her nose twitching, she continued, "Tomorrow I am going to phone Miss Hickson and insist that she take this horrible creature away from me.

She just did not understand.

'To love someone is to respect them.
If we do not understand someone,
How can we love or respect them.'

And Mildred Horseface simply did not understand the little mentally retarded girl called Trixie. She did her best – sure, but she just did not know how to love and care for a little retarded girl.

That night, she cried herself to sleep. Next morning, she was dead! – died of a massive heart attack. Providence, it seemed, had intervened.

Now, once again they had to find a new home for 7 year old Trixie O'Connor.

Only this time they didn't have far to search.

CHAPTER ELEVEN

Lily Watson was a motherly woman. She had four children, who were all grown up now; moved out of her home and started to build lives of their own.

Lily was a woman who always doted on her husband, Henry. They looked forward to their retirement. Planned to visit here; tour there; travel the world together. But then, one day, Henry dropped down dead with a stroke and that was the end of their plans. Poor Lily!

That was a year ago and now, poor soul, she was left all alone to live in that 'big house' at 21 Baker Street.

She didn't like living alone in that great big mansion, with no-one at home now to love and care for. So when the Peabody Organisation told her they'd found her a little girl, she was over the moon.

She didn't mind a Mongol child – a child with her tongue lolling in and out of her mouth when she tried to speak. That didn't bother her at all. The child was human after all, and Lily Watson (or Lil, as they called her) loved human beings, no matter what shape or form they came in.

The word 'disability' didn't bother her either. As far as she was concerned, it existed in the eyes of the beholder only. 'What the child needed was love. Family love,' she thought, 'and she, Lil, was going to give her that.'

She could see that the child, Trixie, was neglected, bereaved of family love. Her mother, Betty O'Connor, had long given up visiting her, because she couldn't cope with the demand made on her. And her poverty-stricken brothers and sisters were struggling with their own survival, never mind coming anywhere near her.

Shunted around like a piece of luggage from one guardian to the next, little Trixie O'Connor was certainly deprived of love, stability and family life and Lily Watson was determined to give her that.

Shocked, that at the age of seven the child was still wetting herself (still wearing nappies) she set about to toilet train her, the same way she did her own children.

Three or four times a day, she used to sit Trixie on the toilet and coax her, "Now Trixie, do a little wee! A little wee, wee!" she would say, emphasising her words with the movement of her lips. Sometimes, she would rub her nose against Trixie's and go, "A little wee! A little wee wee!" and the child would chuckle and sure enough she would pee straight in the toilet pan.

For weeks, Lil continued the same regime, day and night, coaxing, teasing, egging her on, and sometimes giving her sweets when she used the toilet. Then within four weeks, Trixie stopped wetting herself and Lilly Watson was a happy woman.

Next on the agenda, was to teach Trixie how to count and talk.

"One!" Lil would say, raising one finger in the air.

"Onne!" Trixie would repeat, raising one finger up above her head.

"Two! " Lil would continue, lifting two fingers in the air.

"T-ooh!" Trixie would chant, putting up two fingers.

"Three!" Lil continued.

"Teeh!" Trixie screamed. She was so exited, four fingers went up and Lil showered her with hugs and kisses.

"Four!" Lil egged her on again.

"Foo!" five fingers went up.

"No! No! Four! Four!" Lil asserted, putting four fingers up again. Trixie looked at her tearfully, and four fingers went up this time. Lil gave her another sweet.

"Five!"

"Fe-ee!" Five fingers went up and Lil hugged and cuddled her firmly, both giggling their heads off, happy as two sky larks.

Week after week, Lil taught her, encouraged her, giving her chocolate buttons whenever she got it right and with patience and tolerance, after a few months, Trixie was able to count up to ten and speak a few words, albeit in a limited way. But that didn't bother Lil. As long as Trixie could make herself understood. Lily Watson was a relieved woman.

The next step was to teach her to cross the road.

Lil would stand at the pavement holding Trixie's hand and making gestures she would say, "Now my little one, watch the cars and don't cross until they stop. Now they stop. Now, go! Go! Go!" and she would shove Trixie gently across. Then, when Trixie reached the other side of the road and all was clear, she would shout, "Now, come on, here you are!" prompting her with chocolate buttons. Trixie, taking the hint, would race back over when the cars had stopped, and motherly Lil would dance like a wild turkey.

Week after week they practised and within six months, Trixie was able to cross the road by herself. Now, Trixie could go the corner shop and buy little treats when they ran out and Lil was a proud woman.

Lily Watson didn't know much about mentally retarded children. She'd read a few bits and pieces from the hotchpotch Downs Syndrome organisation, but that didn't help much. All Lily could do was trust her intuition. 'Human kindness and love,' she felt, 'was the way to a child's heart' and for her it worked. Kindness and patience had paid off.

Nowadays, Trixie was dressed in new clothes (no more hand-me-downs). She had many toys to play with and she was learning new things. The child was certainly growing, and mellowing into a happy little girl. But then something happened to change all that. First, her mother Betty died suddenly and next, Lil Watson had to give Trixie up.

Betty O'Connor was only 52 when she died prematurely from poverty and exhaustion, her husband Tom having long gone, shortly after Trixie was taken into care. And now poor Lil had the task of telling Trixie of her mother's death.

Using gestures and a picture of Betty, she tried to break the news gently. Speaking slowly in the dead silence, she tried to explain to Trixie about her mother's death until at last, Trixie got the message.

She wept a little, but soon forgot, for her retarded mind could not retain things for long.

It was just as well, poor soul, and Lily Watson breathed a sigh of relief. But sweet Lil had something more pressing on her mind to tell Trixie. A double shock it would be, and that wasn't going to prove to be easy.

Lily Watson had met a wonderful man, an ex-naval officer and at 60, she was going to Australia to start a new life. Lil was a woman who was not prepared to spend the rest of her life alone without a partner, so she would sell her mansion if she had to, and move away with him.

That was fine, but he didn't want a little Mongol girl trailing the outback with them. So Trixie O'Connor had to go.

Poor Lil! Sweet, motherly Lil! How was she going to break the news to the little Mongol girl who had just lost her mother. She was an orphan, poor mite! And Lily Watson just couldn't tell her that she was going to lose her too – the sweet motherly woman they called Lil.

She'd nurtured the child; taught her so many things; grown to love her; watched her mellow and grow into the happy little girl she was and now she had to send her away?

She felt sick, queasy inside, but somehow she knew she had to tell the little girl… break the news as gently as she could…

Tell the little Mongol girl, Trixie… that she, Lil was leaving her for good.

CHAPTER TWELVE

Betty O'Connor was used to poverty. She was born in it she lived in it and she died in it. First, it was her mother Enid, her father Jonas and their 10 kids. But even before that, their grandparents Joshua and Moriah Murphy and their 7 children, almost drowned in it.

Oh! How it left its mark on her!

When she was alive, she often told the story of 'how when she was a child, her father Jonas used to march the street for hours, looking for work.' Up and down he went, backwards and forwards he trotted, looking, looking. Building work; dock work; digging; anything; so that he could feed his 10 children. But he always came home with the same old answer, "No hands needed."

Day after day, he would trail the streets and night after night he would return home to Enid and say, "No work Mah. No work today." The distressed Enid had no choice but to take in washing at 2d a load, in order to subsidise their meagre income of 25shillings a week from Outdoor Relief.

Sometimes, Betty and her brother Artie, used to scour London's dirty streets, scavenging for anything they could find to eat or sell. Often, they would go down the river banks and pick up any scrap, coal; wood; metal; clothes; anything they could sell as street sellers, to try and make ends meet.

But their father, Jonas, couldn't take it. For, when he did manage to find a few days work, he would soon fritter the money away, drowning his sorrows, drinking, gambling or dog-fighting. That was the man he'd turned into.

And so, with little money, they hardly ever managed to hold down a home of their own. On they shuttled, from place to place, room to room. On they moved, all 12 of them often sleeping in one room or two, a rent of 5shillings or so. Jonas, Enid and their 10 children barely survived. Poor souls!

From St Giles to Clerknwell they moved, trying to avoid the Workhouse, living in ramshackle houses surrounded by foul ditches. Rooms so small, so filthy, they could barely breathe; dirt smeared on walls; garbage rotting in heaps outside; barefooted ill-clad children swarming in and out of narrow alleyways, their flaxen hair hanging over their pale faces like damp clouds on a wet night. Oh! How they suffered. On and on, they shifted. From town to town, from room to room they moved. In suffocating poverty, in stinking hell-holes. The family barely surviving.'

Then, there was the story her mother Enid used to tell her about her grandparents, Moriah and Joshua Murphy. 'How they came to England in the 1850s to escape a life of wretched poverty back home in Ireland, only to find themselves sinking into a poverty trap far greater than the one they had left behind.

'With no money and no home of their own, on they moved, from Bethnal Green to Nottingdale. Joshua was a lucky man if he did find work for even two days a week, so that he could feed his 7 kids. He too, used to trail the streets looking for work. Brick making, hod-carrying; anything but nothing much ever materialised.

Close to canals, in working class enclaves they lived, Joshua and his clan; foul contaminating lakes from which clay was dug out to make bricks. They were lucky their children did not die of cholera or whooping cough – with no running water, just buckets-full of contaminated water for their daily use. But they survived. Somehow they did survive.

And that photo was printed so well in Betty's memory.– The photo of Grandma Moriah, which she hung on her bedroom wall; a picture that she used to describe so well, when she was alive. A picture of a short, stout woman in a gown of coarse wool, sodden with sweat; a tattered white apron hanging from her waist; underneath a was short ragged petticoat which covered a pair of strong ankles; large feet clad in dirty white socks; muddy boots, worn out and shapeless and a coarse, black shawl hanging from her tired, aching shoulders.

Over and over, Betty used to tell that story of old Grandma Moriah, how she worked so hard, she and Grandpa Joshua, how they suffered so much, moving from place to place, room to room, trying to avoid their worst fate – the drudgery of the Poor house.

On Outdoor Relief of 2shillings a week, they were lucky if they could pay their rent of 2 or 3shillings a week. And so, they were often forced out. Sometimes all 9 of them sleeping in one room, sharing sanitary facilities with other families. And that was, if they were lucky enough to find a room in the first place.

Grandma Moriah used to work hard in the sweat-shops, making clothes for the rich so that she could earn an extra bob or two, to help feed her children, whilst they scrounged around the dirty stinking streets for anything they could find to sell. Their daughter, Enid often sold flowers on the street, at penny a bunch, but then, as fate would have it, Betty too often had to sell flowers for her survival.

The Murphy clan hawked and sweated, sweated and hawked, Joshua, often in despair, biding his time in beer shops or simply tossing coins in the gambling dens, returning home, most evenings, stinking drunk.

They couldn't pay their rent, Joshua and his family, so on they moved, living in stifling lanes encrusted in human excretions; troops of pale children nestling on muddy steps; families huddled together shivering through the cold, dismal nights.'

That was then, but now, 95 years on and things hadn't changed much, it seemed. Betty and Tom O'Connor suffered the same degrading fate. With 7 kids to feed and no work to be had, all they faced was wretched, stinking poverty.

From generation to generation, it followed them. History had repeated itself, it seemed.

Poor Betty! What a life!

And now at 52, she, Betty O'Connor was dead. Gone forever. And Lil was going away too, to start a new life in Australia, leaving the 8 year old orphan, Trixie, all alone in the world.

And so, once again, the little mentally retarded girl Trixie, was left in the hands of the Peabody Organisation, which they hoped would find her somewhere to live.

CHAPTER THIRTEEN

She was all alone – the little mentally retarded girl. The one they called Trixie. With no-one to love her, no-one to care for her and no-one to give her a steady home.

On and on they moved her, from place to place, from home to home; her face just didn't seem to fit.

Her guardians barely tolerated her. Scrubbing steps, mopping floors, she laboured on and all she could do was cry and cry, 'just another day in paradise.'

She longed for someone to love her, offer her a welcoming smile, extend the width of their open arms and then, along came Lil. But soon, she too had deserted her.

Her last guardian, Rosie, was an improvement on them all. She'd noticed the girl Trixie, was soiling her clothes each time she had her monthly periods, so she spent hours teaching her how to use a sanitary towel and how to change it.

'"This is blood," Rosie used to say, showing her the blood-stained sanitary towel. "Every month, you will soil your pads. You must come and see me when you see a spot of blood on your knickers and I will show you how to use the pad."

"Ye-ah, Ye-ah! Ye-ah, Ye-ah," Trixie would reply, nodding her head, but it wasn't long before she forgot.

"And I will show you how to change it too," Rosie continued. "You mustn't wait until it's wringing with blood. You must change it when it's soaked a little. Do you understand Trixie?"

"Ye-ah, ye-ah! Ye-ah, ye-ah," Trixie would agree, but she soon forgot.

Poor soul! Her retarded memory could not retain information for long.

She never managed to change the pad on time; blood always smearing her skirt or trousers before she got round to changing it and then she would leave it lying on Rosie's clean bathroom floor.

Rosie used to get mad. Again and again, she would teach her, but Trixie never got it right and Rosie was getting fed up to the teeth.

Sometimes when Rosie took her to the supermarket shopping, she would get quite distressed when people stared at the youngster, Trixie, whose tongue lolled in and out of her mouth when she tried to speak. It was as though she was some kind of monster from out of space and Rosie felt very sad.

And so it went. Poor Trixie! Until one day Rosie lost her bearing.

The frequent blocking of Rosie's toilet with toilet rolls and the regular finds of dirty sanitary towels on her clean bathroom floor was more than she could handle. She had reached the end of the line and so decided to phone the Social Visitor and ask her to take Trixie away from her for good. She picked up the phone and dialled…

"Hello Miss Hickson?"

"Miss Denton here, Susannah Denton! Miss Hickson has moved to a different department. Can I help you?"

"Yes, Miss Denton. Yes!… Yes!… of course you can!… "Rosie Millard stuttered, her voice trembling so much you could hardly hear her.

"Rosie? Rosie? Are you there Rosie?"

"Yes! Yes! Miss Denton, Yes!… You see I…"

"Rosie?"

"Yes Miss Denton. You see I, I've had enough of Trixie. I… cannot cope any more. Would you please come and take her away?"

The distressed Rosie told Miss Denton all about Trixie's behaviour and she listened in earnest.

Shocked, she paused for a moment, but then, listening to Rosie's distraught voice she knew the woman could take no more. She was already aware of Trixie's disruptive behaviour and so it came as no big surprise.

She knew she had to make alternative arrangements and she had to do it fast. But that was not going to pose a problem for she already had someone on the books waiting.

"Sure Rosie. Sure!" she assured the distraught woman." I have a lady ready and waiting to take Trixie in. I'll be down tomorrow morning, 10am sharp. Is that OK?"

"Yes Miss Denton, yes. That would be fine."

Rosie put the phone down and wondered how anyone would want to take Trixie in. But then?… she dismissed the thought from her mind.

'One more day,' she thought, 'and that dreadful creature Trixie would be out of her life for good.' She was so relieved.

It was June 1960. Pamela Hickson was gone and Susannah Denton had found a new guardian for 15 year old Trixie O'Connor. The distressed teenager had overheard much of the conversation of Rosie Millard. She was retarded, she couldn't speak much, but she understood a lot of what was said and she was left deeply disturbed.

She started to cry. Sobbed her heart out and no-one heard her, it seemed.

But somewhere in the distance someone did hear her. That someone was Marjorie Pinkerton, a 52 year old music teacher from Green Acres. She was ready and waiting to take Trixie in.

CHAPTER FOURTEEN

44 Green Acres was a sumptuous dwelling. Set in almost an acre of green land high up on the hills, this detached Tudor-styled cottage, with its white-washed walls, framed by dark wooden panels and low-beamed ceilings, stood out from the rest. Hanging baskets with blossoming blue violets and yellow pansies adorned its walls; silver-coloured ivy trailing down its sides; a gravel driveway with eye-catching borders of daffodils and crocuses, dancing in the wind. An air of Tudor opulence. It was a picturesque sight indeed!

Handed down to her from her mother when she died, it was a home which savoured many wonderful memories for Marjorie Pinkerton: memories of an idyllic childhood; of feeding the swans in the nearby lake and watching them cruise along, their majestic necks stretched out like miniature boats sailing the river. Skipping, jumping, running; laughing at the ducks – these were the pictures that lived on in Marjorie's imagination; pictures that she was to cherish for the rest of her life.

She went to school from there; trained to be a teacher from there; all good things happened to her there, in that all-embracing homely cottage.

She remembered the extravagant musical evenings they used to have, when her mother played the piano, her father being home on leave from his Command in the Middle East.

Friends and relations would drop in for Sunday lunch, then the music and fun would start. They would hum along, sing tunes: anything from Frank Sinatra to Nina Simone – most of them singing way out of tune. Then, simultaneously, they would burst into fits of laughter, laughing… laughing their heads off; the cottage erupting into spasms of gaiety.

Yes, those were magic days indeed, but then the blow came when one day her mother died suddenly of a heart attack; her father following shortly after, having been blown up by an Arab bomb.

That was a year ago and Marjorie Pinkerton never got over the shock. Now, here she was, alone, trapped in this bewildering cottage with memories that would haunt her; memories of an idyllic childhood, yet, which ended so tragically for her parents.

Marjorie Pinkerton grieved a lot.

She never liked living alone. Her life was always filled with people, so when the Peabody Organisation told her they had found her a 15 year old Mongol girl to care for, she was blissfully happy.

She had heard about the traumatic life this little Mongol girl, Trixie O'Connor, had endured and was determined to try and heal the pain. As a teacher, she would teach the youngster, teach her new skills; teach her anything she wished to learn.

She herself had an idyllic childhood; an enchanting adolescence; exciting womanhood; idyllic everything, almost, and she Marjorie Pinkerton, was determined to project that enchanting lifestyle to any child who came into her care.

She would give the child a good life; she was sure. The best she could muster.

And so, Marjorie began her journey of discovery. Coaxing and teaching, with gentle persuasion and human kindness, within a few months of her stay there, Trixie O'Connor had learnt to change her sanitary pads on time. And she was putting them in the sanitary bin too, not on Marjorie's newly-scrubbed bathroom floor.

Sometimes, Marjorie would take Trixie to the supermarket, shopping. She had learnt that Trixie liked baked beans, rice-pudding, ice cream and crisps, so she used to teach her, encourage her to find these goods for herself and place them in the shopping trolley. Then, she would give her the money to pay for it all at the check-out counter and also collect the change, whilst she stood behind her, watching, coaxing and encouraging.

Trixie couldn't count any more than 10, Marjorie knew that, but it didn't matter. All she wanted was for Trixie to learn a little at a time, grow in confidence and she was there to help her. And so, when Trixie got it right, Marjorie would say, "You've done it! You've done it! Well done! Well done!" and she would give her a coin and hug her and they would both giggle away like two young kids.

Another feature of Trixie's new life with Marjorie was musical evenings. Just like the days of her own childhood, musical evenings were becoming part of their regular life together.

Being a Christian person, Marjorie would pound away at the piano playing tunes like 'When you walk through a storm... and don't be afraid of the dark...' and Trixie would sit on the Heppleworth chair, listening in earnest, drumming away on the polished, lace-topped Chippendale table, drumming...drumming... chuckling away. Then Marjorie would continue, 'Amazing grace, how sweet thou art... to find me a special little girl...' (Marjorie often added her own bits to these songs) and Trixie would get excited and chant "aa-ah, aa-ah... ee-eh, ee-eh... te-ah... te-eh ee-eh..." swinging her head, chanting, chanting... way out of tune, Marjorie loving every moment of it.

She could see the teenager was enjoying the music, every note of it and she was determined to do something about it. Yes. She was going to get Trixie a little guitar for her birthday and teach her how to play it.

Then, the big day came.

It was Sunday 17th October, Trixie's 16th birthday and people were buzzing about preparing a grand supper.

The polished dining table was highly decorated – silver cutlery, polished to a sheen; exotic Royal Doulton dishes; shimmering glasses; pink silver-edged serviettes skilfully laid out; silver candelabras carefully arranged; exquisite bowls of flowers placed with style along the centre of the table; the strong smell of coffee brewing in the percolator, back in the kitchen.

It was to be a special day and so Marjorie had hired a French chef to cook and serve them with food she knew Trixie would enjoy. For starters, they had cream of chicken soup, then came fish and chips cooked French style; followed by ice-cream topped with strawberry sauce and finally they were served with well-brewed coffee laced with a thick film of cream.

Next, it was time for the cake – soft sponge topped with pink icing upon which stood 16 lighted candles.

"Happy Birthday to you…" they sang, as the chef brought the cake in. "Happy Birthday dear Trixie…" they continued, all six of them. The chef joined in, "Blow de candel, Trixie, Blow! Blow! Blow…!

Trixie blew and blew. It took all but four efforts to blow them out and they laughed their heads off. They giggled and chanted, whistled and hooted, Trixie, bellowing away with them. An atmosphere of almost bacchanalian spirit echoed through the winds of this opulent cottage as Trixie started to examine her presents; a moment of silence when Marjorie walked in and handed Trixie her present – a specially adapted guitar.

Excited, Trixie jumped out of her chair and started strumming straight away, hopelessly out of tune whilst Marjorie thumped away at the piano. She was playing the Beatle's hit songs, making up her own words as she went along. "Shake it up Trixie now…" and they went, "Twist and shout" – Trixie strumming away haphazardly, singing. "Tra-ah, Tra-ah, Aa-ah, Aa-ah…"

It was like a comic scene from a hilarious movie.

But Trixie could not play. All she was doing was banging away at the strings and Marjorie knew she had to help her.

She would use her skills as a teacher, teach her how to play. It would be trying, she knew, but the youngster loved that guitar, she could see that now. And if the child could learn to play it properly, she would be able to join in with her friends at the local church.

Marjorie Pinkerton was going to teach Trixie, the little Mongol girl, new skills and ho! How she was glad.

She was going to help the youngster to live as full a life as possible, but before she could do so, there was something else she had to do.

Trixie was 16, but she was well below that age in her behaviour, in grasping and learning new things. The first thing she must do was to get the Psychologist to assess Trixie. Then she could start to teach the child to play.

Two weeks later, she did. The result: Trixie O'Connor was 16 but she had a mental age of 9.

If she was to teach Trixie to play the guitar, then she must teach her as she would a 9 year old. She must therefore work out a teaching plan accordingly.

CHAPTER FIFTEEN

Marjorie knew that as a retarded girl, Trixie's thought process was slow, impaired in some way. She could learn some things, sure, but it had to be in simplified form, one step at a time and at her own pace. So Marjorie Pinkerton set out to do just that.

As an experienced teacher, she knew that Trixie could not read nor write, but she could understand the alphabet (at least part of it) in a phonetic way and she could also count up to 10 – Lily and Rosie had taught her that. So Marjorie set about teaching Trixie just the way she should – one step at a time.

She started, by sticking the numbers 1 to 10 on the bottom end of each string of the guitar. Then she stuck corresponding ones on each note of her music sheet. Then it was time for her to begin to teach: "1…" "Doh…" she sang, placing Trixie's finger on the appropriate numbered string. Trixie twiddling away; "2!…"… "Ray…" "3!…" "Me…" "4!"… "Fah…" "5!…" So…" "6!"… "Lah…" and so it went, over and over she coaxed. "Come on Trix," she would say, egging her on.

Week after week they practised, Trixie banging away at the strings, she hugging and kissing Trixie each time she got it right. Until slowly but surely, Trixie began to master all 8 strings – 8 notes, 8 strings. It was not a lot, but it was a start.

'Now she could join her musician friends at the church,' Marjorie thought, and her heart brimmed with joy.

When Trixie first started going to church, she used to sit on a table at the back, doodling, chuckling, making noises, anything to attract her attention and distract from the service. But as soon as the band came on, she used to get so excited, that she would cock her ears up to listen and make gestures as if she was leading the band herself, and Father Donahue used to wink at her, mischievously.

But nowadays, things were different. Now, she could play. And so, whenever the musicians played, she would start strumming away at her guitar and Father Donahue used to look at her with interest. Then one day, Marjorie decided to approach him and he agreed to let her join the band.

Things were changing for Trixie now. Now, she could join in the band, play her guitar and she was almost jumping for joy. Now, she had something to look forward to and so she began to take more interest in the church services.

Every Sunday she would come in early, sometimes well before Marjorie. Often, she would tidy up the place, clean the seats, dust it here, dust it there. Then, she would stand at the front, greeting everyone unceremoniously as they came in. But they didn't mind. They were pleased to see the little Mongol girl, growing and developing her self-confidence, especially Father Donahue. He watched with interest.

And so, it was no surprise that after six months, with some cajoling from Marjorie, he agreed to let Trixie become a sides-person: handing out service books, taking up collection plates, tidying up after the Service. Now, Trixie was being recognised as a teenager in her own rights and Marjorie was a happy woman.

"One of the most important things," Father Donahue asserted during one of his sermons, "Is to greet people with friendliness as they come in, and who better to do that than Trixie. We all know too, that one of the hardest parts of being a Christian is to love they neighbour and she genuinely loves people – race, colour, creed or class does not come into it – everyone is a friend, and this friendliness is returned a thousand-fold. Trixie O'Connor is an example to us and we must cherish that," he concluded and there was a hush amongst the audience.

For Trixie, life was moving on.

First, he allowed her to join the band, then, she was made a sides-person and now these kind words too! And sometimes, when he passed by her, dressed in his golden robes and mitre, he used to wink at her, give her a smile and she would chuckle with joy and Marjorie would smile too, but it didn't end there. The teaching programme continued.

"Onwards Christian soldiers," Marjorie would chant and Trixie would strum away, cackling like a wild hyena. Sometimes, she would get it wrong, but Marjorie didn't mind. Patience was something she had in abundance.

She was always there, Marjorie, watching, coaxing, encouraging, and assessing Trixie on her strength and personality, not on her weakness. She respected her struggle to gain some independence and flinched from demonstrating her love towards the growing youngster.

Sometimes, when Trixie got it right, Marjorie would give her treats (rewards) in the form of items of new clothing. And so in an atmosphere of love, the youngster grew, developed and learnt many things. She learnt how to set the table, fold napkins, tidy her room, do the laundry, make tea or coffee and even took pride in her appearance, developing a funny dress sense. She even learnt to say a few words in a limited way, but at least she could talk.

One day, tired from a hard day's teaching, Marjorie dropped weightily on the sofa. She was just nodding off when, 'Ding! Dong! Ding! Dong!' the little hand bell went. It was Trixie, carrying a tray of tea and biscuits for Marjorie.

"What a pleasant surprise?" Marjorie declared, as Trixie put the tray down and started pouring out the tea. Marjorie, the guardian angel, watched Trixie, her charge, as she poured the tea with care. She was taken back by the warm and caring human being Trixie was developing into.

Then, when she was nearly 17, there came a further surprise.

One day, Father Donahue visited and told Marjorie that he would like Trixie to appear in the next church play. It was such a shock but Marjorie Pinkerton was over the moon.

"Trixie?" she accosted her when she entered the front parlour. "Father Donahue was here. He would like you to take part in the next church play."

With gestures and signs and holding up a colourful coat, she managed to relay to Trixie what the play was about and Trixie chuckled like a monkey about to get a bunch of bananas. She was so happy. Then, as luck would have it, Marjorie was chosen to teach the cast.

"No, No! Not so!" she asserted when she was teaching them. "Like this! Like this!" she went. "Straighten your knees Bobby," she went. Then, "Open your mouth Sandra; let the vowels out like this, "Ooh…! Aah…!" Trixie doubling up into fits of laughter, heedlessly strumming away, getting most of the tunes wrong.

"What an opportunity!…" Marjorie declared… "Too good to miss. I must tell Miss Denton," and without wasting much time, she was on the phone.

"Miss Denton? Marjorie Pinkerton here."

"Hello, Miss Pinkerton."

"Miss Denton, I have exciting news for you."

"Exciting? Oh!…"

"Yes Miss Denton. Remember your last visit, you were so impressed about the way Trixie was developing? Well, I have better news for you."

"News. Oh?…"

"Yes Miss Denton, exciting news. You see, Trixie is appearing in the next church play.

Marjorie Pinkerton did not waste any more time. In her excitement, she reeled off all the information about the play: the date, the time, the venue, the cast, everything while Miss Denton listened excitedly. They were like a couple of women anticipating a hen party.

Then finally the big day came.

Gleaming in their different coloured costumes, the actors entered and left the stage, reciting, talking, and singing to the audience. Suddenly, the lights went dim, then, as if with the stroke of a match, the spotlight shone, showering its bright beams unto the central character, as he walked in, wearing his Colourful Coat, strumming away on his guitar.

It was Trixie.

The audience went mad. They stood up, whistling, hooting. "Come on Trixie! Come on!" they shouted. "Give us some more. More! More!" they screamed, clapping and whistling. They blew and hooted, whistled and clapped. Trixie chuckling and strumming away at her guitar, getting it wrong sometimes, but they didn't notice. Then, she took her bow as Marjorie had taught her to and left the stage, leaving Miss Denton in tears.

Now it was time for the feast to start and what an evening it was; an evening Marjorie Pinkerton did not wish to forget; an evening she wanted to treasure for the rest of her life – the photos being a constant reminder of the day, her charge, the little Mongol girl Trixie O'Connor, came out on her own.

For years she'd watched the youngster mellow, from a little mentally retarded backward girl – a girl who was once written off as useless when she first came to her; to the woman she was now. Now, here she was, able to do so many things on her own like tie her own shoe laces, button her coat and hang it in its place and play the guitar too! Oh! How she blossomed into a woman; a woman with character, and a style of her own.

'So many of her actions that once seemed meaningless had taken on a significance of their own now and showed that there was a logical person behind the speechless child. There was no glib answer to the problems she experienced. It yielded its own fruit of personal growth,' Marjorie thought.

Marjorie Pinkerton began to cry. She was crying, not just tears of sadness, but of joy; joy of the lone girl who was once so bereft, but who had now come of age, shining, in a style of her own.

When she had taught her how to keep her surroundings tidy, she had given her a special pillowcase in which to store the little things that she treasured: comb; eye-glasses (which she soon threw away); pieces of wool to wrap into balls; toilet paper; a duster to clean with and sweets and chocolate buttons in a special little box.

There was logic to Marjorie's thinking; a pillowcase, because it was easier to handle and carry around, instead of a complicated handbag with its rusty old zipper and funny unmanageable buttons. And Trixie learned to love that pillowcase.

It had become part of her. She clung to it. She carried it with her wherever she went – sometimes, chuckling away to herself.

She was the happiest person on earth.

But then, as fate would have it, all good things must come to an end, or so it seemed. Marjorie Pinkerton collapsed with a stroke one day and was left paralysed down one side of her body. She also lost her speech and within a week she was dead! Gone forever.

And now they had to find a new home for Trixie O'Connor.

Homeless, penniless and loveless, the 25 year old retarded woman, the one they called Trixie, was once again on the move. This time taking with her, a shapeless white pillowcase containing her belongings – 'sad-rags and glad-rags' –the only things she had left in the whole wide world.

CHAPTER SIXTEEN

It was a cold winter's morning, when Susannah Denton and Trixie O'Connor made their way to 99 Mercy Farm, a tall imposing building standing all alone, high on top of a hill.

A bleak Victorian house, it stood there, ghost-like, detached, towering high above other buildings, like a keeper, keeping watch over its flock. Grey stoned walls under a dark slated roof; wind howling through gaping holes left there by fallen slates; grey stoned steps and a well-trodden path from a courtyard bereft of plants, of life, barren but for the one car parked in the far corner of this deserted yard.

Inside, winding, stoned stairways led from one area of the bleak house to the next: from kitchen to storeroom, from bathroom to laundry, winding, winding, like a spider's web. Enclosed bedrooms designed to keep the inmates in, it seemed. A commanding building, it was. Two dilapidated houses joined together, haphazardly.

In the bedrooms, walls stood out, bereft of colour, almost dead; no pictures, no personal touches, just plain whitewashed walls in all 10 of them; overcrowded rooms, designed to house 10 inmates. Instead, it housed 15.

'Plain whitewashed walls, easier to keep clean – keep the ghosts away.' That was how Miss McCorkindale described it, when Miss Denton visited the place prior to Trixie's admission. But Miss Denton took no notice of what was said at the time. It didn't dawn on her, what she was getting herself and Trixie into.

And now, here they were waiting in the cramped cold office of Mercy Farm, waiting to see the Head of the home, Miss Joyce McCorkindale – a grand name for a grand lady. Though their appointment was 10am, they arrived half an hour early, so that Trixie could settle into her new home before Miss Denton departed – But Miss McCorkindale kept them waiting.

She was a stickler for timekeeping: a few minutes late or a few minutes early and the appointee was kept toeing the line. Now, there she was keeping them in check. She was far too important and much too busy to rush.

They sat there waiting patiently, when, all of a sudden they heard, 'click, clock! Click, clock!' the heels of her shoes were clicking, as she made her way through the winding staircase, towards them. It was exactly 10am on the dot when she appeared.

A tall, slim woman, immaculately dressed, not a hair out of place; with an elongated face and thin pointed nose, she looked more like a wax doll than a person who was to take charge of other human beings.

"Good morning, Miss Denton," she greeted, coarsely. "I hope you had a safe journey here." Then, turning brusquely to Trixie, she added, "Well. Hello young lady... and how are you? I see you are looking well, Miss...?" She didn't even bother to shake their hands.

"Trixie! Trixie O'Connor!" Susannah Denton stepped in to intercept her.

"Yes... Yes! Of course!... I should have known... it's all here in the folder," Miss McCorkindale apologised anxiously, fixing her gaze on Trixie, but refraining from disclosing too much.

"And now Trixie, we must get down to formalities." She was determined to assert her authority.

"Breakfast is at 8am sharp. You are called at 6am. You must get washed, dressed and be in the dining room by 7.50am. That gives you enough time to be seated and ready to be served. No horsing around. No fighting for each other's seat. Is that understood?"

"A-ah, aa-ah! A-ah, aa-ah!" Trixie nodded in agreement, tongue bobbing in and out of her mouth as she tried to speak. "Ye-ah, ye-ah... Ye-ah, ye-ah!" she acquiesced.

Behind the door, two persons were listening – they were Frankie and Jonnie. "She getting de drill, she getting de drill," they whispered, thumping each other on the shoulder. "Ha Ha! Ha, Ha!" they laughed, horsing around with each other.

But no one heard them.

"And!... Miss McCorkindale continued, "My girls always look smart. No wearing of un-ironed clothes and no stockings crinkling down the ankles either. Understood Trixie? Understood?"

Trixie didn't understand, but she agreed. "Ye-ah, ye-ah! Ye-ah, ye-ah!" she went.

Miss McCorkindale shifted a little, then, looking at Trixie from above the top of her horn-rimmed spectacles, hanging precariously from the bridge of her nose, she continued to reel out the laws. With precision, she read on: the rest of the meal times; the do's and don'ts; the rules of the home. No holes barred.

All the while, Frankie and Jonnie were behind the door, listening. Jumping with joy, they giggled away, unashamedly.

"And now for the chores," Miss McCorkindale continued, asserting her authority. "Your job, Trixie, is to lay the dining room table, clean the dining room floor and help in the kitchen when needed. I understand you like kitchen work. Yes?..."

"Ye-ah, ye-ah! Ye-ah, ye-ah!" Trixie agreed, excitedly. She was ready to jump from the chair, straight away and start laying the table. For, when she was with Marjorie, she used to take pride in doing that job. She liked to watch the silver cutlery shimmering away on the gleaming white tablecloth. But right now, she had to listen, take instructions from the Boss, Miss McCorkindale. The woman they called, Mam.

When they heard that, Frankie and Jonnie cocked their ears up. "She got to work. She got to work," they squeaked together. "Dat go pu' 'er in 'er place." But they were not too happy.

"Well, that's all for now Trixie," Miss McCorkindale concluded. Then, turning abruptly to Miss Denton, she added,

"You've got my telephone number, Miss Denton. Feel free to phone me anytime," and as quick as a mouse, she was up on her feet, ready to show Miss Denton the door.

Susannah Denton was not too happy. 'This woman, reeling all the rules out, asserting her authority!' And she wasn't sure whether Trixie understood much either, or whether she could retain it in her memory for long, but there was not a lot she could do right now.

During the post-war days, times were hard. Many families had lost their loved ones and were only too glad to take in a Mongol person, if only to earn a bob or two. But now, in the '70s, people had prospered and they didn't want to take in retarded people anymore. So, the Peabody Organisation had to turn to private institutions to take in their charges – springing up all over the place, they were – charging a fat fee and getting rich.

And so now, Susannah Denton had to say her 'good-byes,' leaving Trixie O'Connor, one of 15 inmates, in the charge of a woman they called Mam, in an antiquated home named Mercy Farm, under the treacherous and foxy eyes of two half-witted women called Frankie and Jonnie.

They had been there long enough, these two. Earned their privileges and rewards, got their quasi-official status and no-one was going to take that away from them.

They'd spied. They'd listened. They had heard it all and they didn't like that cute-cat with her pretty clothes and guitar strung around her neck.

She was dumb, they were sure; couldn't talk, they knew that; so it wouldn't be that difficult to put her through the 'initiation process' – put her through the grind.

Mam had given her the 'drill' but they, Frankie and Jonnie, had much more in store.

CHAPTER SEVENTEEN

They had made up their minds.

They were buddies and some even called them the Dyad. They'd built up excellent methods of persuasion in that rickety home with its quasi-ranking line of status and no-one was going to take that away from them.

Frankie, who saw herself as leader, used to take in Mam's dinner to her everyday, in the office. All laid out sprucely on a tray, it was: shining silver cutlery; crisp white linen serviettes folded neatly in silver rings; floral china plates and pretty china teacups for her tea. It was a special privilege accorded to her. 'And now simple-minded female Trixie, wit' her tongue hangin' out, was given job so nar de kichen! She will take away oor prifilege, if she can.' Frankie thought. 'Dat was too close foor comfort.'

"We ca-arn let dat happen." Jonnie asserted. "She go fine out oor secret and pinch oor favour!"

"No we ca'rn," Frankie agreed. "We got to do sometin, got to do sometin!" she insisted, her face taunt as a cracked, hard-boiled egg. Stamping, stamping her feet she was.

A big woman, Frankie was, almost forty and when she walked she moved with a spring like a lion. Her strong, heavy steps gliding forwards with certainty. Her big legs moving onwards, one in front of the other, and her skirt rustling in the air. She was so large, anyone who passed by had to give way – they were afraid of her.

To look at her, her face seemed normal, like any other woman really – no sign of Mongolism, it seemed. But if you closed your eyes, you would see – through your mind's eye – a vision of a big lion leaping, leaping forward, stalking with precision, about to jump on its prey.

But she was retarded alright; this self-appointed leader and most people were scared of her; all but Jonnie.

Jonnie was her best friend – her soul mate.

The situation with Jonnie was similar.

In your mind's eye you could see the vision of a fox, dark cagey eyes, darting here, darting there, all over the place. With long narrow jaws and shifty eyes, this skinny woman was two years younger than Frankie, but together, they made the perfect duo; she keeping watch most of the time, whilst Frankie led the hunt.

She too looked normal, but she was nuts alright. The things she got up to. Mam only had to be firm and she would cry like a child. Beg for forgiveness.

The perfect pair they were, those two. And now they had a job to do.

They would break Trixie's will; break her spirits by any means they could. Let her know that only they, the Dyad could carry 'buddy status,' get special privileges. They would put her down; keep her there, if they could.

And so the plan was hatched.

One day while Trixie was walking along the corridor, they tripped her over. She fell with a bang! Bruised her nose and cut her lips.

That was soon put right with a special dressing Mam had applied, but when Mam questioned them they said Trixie had tripped over and fell and Mam believed them.

"Is no good," Jonnie asserted. "We got to do sometin' worse. Ca-rn you see, Mam only like 'er more."

"Ye-ah, Ye-ah!" Frankie agreed, "but wha?" She was thinking, thinking, then all of a sudden it came…

Rumour had it that Trixie used to block the toilet with toilet rolls – it's amazing how rumours flourish in such a hole. And so, now Frankie had something to work on…"Look" she blurted, we go bloc de toilet wit toilet roll an' tel Mam, Trixie done it."

"Huh huh. Huh, huh!" Jonnie laughed. "Dat go fix 'er." Mam go mad an' you kno' what?"… She didn't finish the sentence.

"Hah hah! Hah hah!" they giggled together, each nudging the other; each understanding the next stage of the game.

They didn't have to wait long. A couple of weeks later and it was time for action.

Every day, between 1-2pm after lunch, most of the residents used to nod off and the two duty staff used to be on their breaks, chatting away or reading magazines. Now they were ready for action – the perfect time for these two to stalk their prey. It was so easy; no-one would see them.

One of Jonnie's chores was to replenish the inmates' toiletries. And so on this day, at siesta time, she sprang into motion. Quietly, she crept into Millie's bedroom and stole her toilet roll. Then together, she and Frankie stalked the corridor, stepped into Mam's toilet and quickly rammed the toilet roll down the toilet hole. They rammed and rammed until it was well and truly blocked, then quietly tiptoed out, as stealthily as two blind mice.

Later that day, when Mam went to use the toilet she found it blocked. She went mad!

"It's Trixie, it's Trixie Mam!" they both squealed together. "We see ' er do it Mam, we see'er doin' it!"

Miss McCorkindale (Mam) lost no time. She summoned Trixie to the office straight away.

"Trixie, why did you block the toilet?" she stormed, her eyes flashing as if on fire.

"N-a-h, n-a-h. N-a-h, n-a-h!" Trixie cried, her head shaking from side to side. She was scared.

In fact, ever since Trixie went to live with Lily, she'd stopped blocking toilets, but now, no-one believed her. How could they? It was there, written in her Case File and no-one had bothered to change it. And now it had become part of Trixie's history, part of the bureaucratic garbage, stored in that big brown file, ready to summon at a moment's notice.

"You are not to do it, understand Trixie," Mam continued.

"Ye-ah, ye-ah, ye-a!"… Trixie sobbed, Mam looking at her with pity now. She didn't know whether to believe Trixie or not, but she would let her off, at least this time.

Behind the door Frankie and Jonnie were listening. Ears cocked up, they didn't like what they heard.

"She got off," Jonnie said, turning blue with rage.

"Well, ah did me bes'," Frankie replied, "wat else can we do. We go get caut?"

"Oh no we won' " Jonnie squeaked, her foxy eyes lightening up as she thought and thought… "Ah got it, ah got it!" Jonnie affirmed, almost jumping for joy. "We go bloc de toilet with Miriam's false teet."

"But how you go get Miriam's false teet?"

Jonnie looked at her, a sly grin on her face. Like a fox, she was ready, ready as if waiting to spring on a lone chicken the fox had seen in the distance. And Frankie didn't have to ask any more questions – she knew the answer…

They, the buddies, laid low for a month or so, then the day came for them to spring into action.

It was siesta time and most of the residents were asleep; some snoring their heads off; some drooping; some dribbling; some rocking; some spitting. Every now and then a nose twitched as the television ran riot – lines of waves shooting through its screen as it hissed and whistled out of tune.

As quiet as a mouse, Jonnie crept in. First, she checked that Miriam was asleep, then she checked on Trixie too – she too was gone, head leaning on one side, breathing heavily.

Jonnie sprang into action.

She sneaked into Miriam's room, grabbed her false teeth which were soaking in a pot, wrapped them in tissue paper and crept out of the room. Like a fox, she stood in the corridor, looked around briskly – all was quiet –put two fingers up in the air to indicate to Frankie that all was well, as Frankie was standing there like a guard, keeping watch.

Gingerly, they tiptoed along the stoned corridor, entered the main toilet which was used by most of the residents and dropped the false teeth in the hole. Then, they got some toilet roll and rammed and rammed until the toilet was well and truly blocked.

"Now she go get it," they chuckled together.

At 3pm sharp, they went into Mam's office and told her that they saw Trixie blocking the toilet with Miriam's false teeth. They described the action in such detail, it was if it came straight out of a movie itself. Mam was seething.

Without saying a word, she summoned Trixie to the office.

"Trixie! You have done it again. Blocked the toilet Trixie! Blocked the toilet!"

"N-a-ah, n-a-ah. N-a-ah, n-a-ah!" Trixie pleaded, shaking her head from side to side, tears welling up in her eyes.

Like a school teacher, Mam hammered the words, "Trixie you have stolen Miriam's false teeth and stuffed them down the loo. How could you do such a thing Trixie? How could you?" Mam's face was red with anger.

"Na-ah, n-a-ah! N-a-ah, n-a-ah!" Trixie howled, tears streaming down her cheeks now. She could see the anger on Mam's face and was frightened of what she might do.

"Trixie," Mam continued, wagging her fingers, raging like a bull now. "This is the second time you have done this. This is costing a fortune."

Trixie bent her head, sobbing, sobbing.

"I do not know if the plumber will be able to fix it this time," Mam asserted. "I may have to replace it with a brand new toilet this time and I cannot have that. Understand Trixie! Understand!" Mam's eyes ablaze as she droned on and on…

Trixie shook in her chair.

Behind the door, Frankie and Jonnie were listening, laughing their heads off.

"You have not kept your promise," Mam continued fiercely, her eyes rolling. "You will be punished Trixie, you must be punished!" she asserted, bellowing like a lion now. "You will go out to the front and scrub the stone steps until you can see your face in them. Understand Trixie? Understood Trixie? Understood!"

She leaned forward, staring Trixie straight in the face. "You will scrub and scrub until we call you in. Understood!" And with that she rang the bell and summoned a member of staff to take Trixie to her peril, Trixie sobbing her heart away.

She sobbed and sobbed as she trotted behind the member of staff, her legs weak as two pieces of straw.

Like two wild rabbits, Frankie and Jonnie scuttled, laughing, jumping, and thumping each other wildly. "We got 'er dis time," they howled, rocking with laughter. "Nex' time we go finish 'er fo' good," they seemed certain.

Mam wasn't sure whether Frankie and Jonnie were telling the truth. But that didn't matter. They were important to her and she couldn't lose face with them. If she did, they would stop doing their designated chores and she would have to pay someone else to do them. That would cost her money and she couldn't have that.

She, Mam, was a trained Social Worker, well versed in Social Work theory. Behaviour Modification was her pet thing – it was what she believed in – Reward and punishment was her method.

If a resident did something good, she must be rewarded, given money, treats, like Frankie and Jonnie. But if she did a wrong deed, the only way to put it right was by punishment; only then would she be able to see that she had done something wrong and therefore try to modify her behaviour – try to put it right.

Yes, Mam was a firm believer in Behaviour Modification, the popular theory – the spin theory she'd learnt from the system and so now, Trixie had to be punished.

Now, once again, Trixie O'Connor was shunted out into the cold, scrubbing steps, crying out to anyone who would hear her plea.

CHAPTER EIGHTEEN

Frankie and Jonnie were as happy as two song birds. They'd worked the system at Mercy Farm and almost bled it dry. They'd climbed the status ladder (quasi though it may have seemed), gained favours in that antiquated asylum and no-one was going to take that away from them now.

Frankie had her own personal territory – a special chair in the Day Room, placed right in front of the television. She used to stuff her handbag full to the brim with food, chocolates, fruit, and soap, anything she could stash and place it firmly on the chair. She'd stake private claim to that chair – A tacit right that no-one dared question. And no-one had the gall to sit on it, or dislodge her belongings either. If they did, there was hell to pay, for she was Frankie the leader and they recognised her right to this territorial jurisdiction.

The inmates therefore learnt how to keep their distance by hard lessons.

Jonnie too, had her assigned place. Her nest was a chair in the corner, stacked with biscuits, sweets, books and cards. Even though she couldn't read she still hoarded these… and anything else she could lay her hands on. And the others knew too well how to keep away from her.

They were even both allowed to use a free-standing radiator. They used to wash their knickers and bras and hang them there to dry. And often, they would stack their stolen stash: face cloth, soap, comb, hairbrush, behind this formidable radiator and no-one ever noticed their hoards, for no-one bothered to check.

There was an unused chair in the corridor. But no inmate dared sit on it, for if they did, Frankie and Jonnie would bawl them out. "Get back to your room! You… Ah go tell Mam you sitin' on de chare..." they used to shout and the frightened inmate would scamper off.

Often, they would force a mute woman off her footstool and take it for themselves. Such was the authority they had gained for themselves, these two women known as the Dyad. The staff would give tacit support to their claims and Mam turned a blind eye to it also.

Yes, these two had built up their stakes alright, claiming special privileges and rights, in return for jobs done. Assignments, they called them. Frankie, working in the kitchen and Jonnie, cleaning, restocking used items in the rooms and helping with the laundry.

So privileged were they that Frankie was given a key to the kitchen storeroom, whilst Jonnie got one to the dry goods store cupboard. Yes, they had worked themselves up in the system alright. And as daft as they were, they'd learnt to play the game well – even saw themselves as members of staff and sane, and the others, daft and insane.

They even learnt how to bide their time until the perfect opportunity, siesta time, came. Then, Frankie would sneak into the storeroom with the key, whilst Jonnie kept watch. She would put two fingers up (the all clear signal) and Frankie would dash in quickly, load her shopping bag – stacking it full with soap; toilet paper; washing powder; face flannels; scouring pads; anything they could sell at the local market.

One day they were stealing from the cupboard, when they heard a sound. "Quick, Quick!" Jonnie whispered. "Someone comin'!" They scampered in the cupboard and shut the door tight, behind them. It was Mam – she went straight past and didn't hear a thing. They waited till it was quiet again then crept out quietly; the shopping bag loaded with goodies, and hid it below Frankie's bed.

They breathed a sigh of relief. At least this time, they didn't get caught.

Another safe period for stealing goods was night-time.

They knew that Josephine the night staff, used to make up a bed and have a good sleep. Sometimes, they would even take her a cup of hot chocolate to help her along. Then, when she was flat out, snoring her head off, they used to sneak into the kitchen store cupboard and steal their stash: packets of tea, sugar, coffee, biscuits, jam, and marmalade; anything in packets that was light and easy to carry. They would cram these into their shopping bag and dart for the bedroom, which they shared.

Jonnie had it all worked out too. Sometimes, when she was cleaning the rooms, she used to steal combs, talcum powder, perfume and even brooches, stuffing them down the tights of her trouser legs, then heading sharply for her room.

As for freebies, often when there were leftovers from the kitchen, these were given to Frankie and Jonnie – jugs of milk, pieces of cake and sandwiches, were given daily to these two, to take to their rooms.

Yes, they were living the life of Riley alright. And to top it all, they were never, ever caught stealing. For, whenever Mam found an item or two missing, they always had an answer for her. They knew the game and they played it well.

One day, Mam summoned them to the office. "Frankie? Jonnie?" Mam questioned. "Two packets of biscuits, one packet of tea and one pound of sugar went missing. Do you know anything about this?"

"No Mam, no," they both squeaked together. "It mus' be use' up, Mam, oh somebody else take it," they asserted together, their squeaky voices giving them away.

Mam looked at them, her eyes shifting from one to the other beneath her dark horn-rimmed spectacles, and then her mind started ticking. 'It must be Josephine,' she thought, and so Josephine, the night staff, promptly became the target of suspicion and Frankie and Jonnie were let off the hook.

Frankie and Jonnie had learnt to play the game and so far, they were playing it well. They were seen as embracing their assignments, but in fact, they were profiting from it. Profiting? Well, they had a system all worked out. They used to trade their stash with Myra O'Keefe, a benevolent lady at the local open market.

They would act as runners too; buy sweets, toiletries etc. for the inmates and get tips or special payments for these – payments often arranged in advance.

Yes, Frankie and Jonnie were doing very well indeed.

They were privileged inmates and so they were given the best, front room with the best view in the home; a room that turned out to be perfect for their lifestyle. For, outside their window was a large butterfly bush – the perfect place to hide their stash; a place from which they operated as the craftiest burglars in town.

Often at night-time, when everyone was asleep, they would ram the stolen goods down a pillowcase or stocking, and open the window slowly and gently. Jonnie would be keeping watch as usual, and then if all was clear, she would whisper, "Quick! Quick! All clear." Then Frankie would slide the pillowcase down the drainpipe, making quite sure it landed behind the bushes. Then they would close the window quietly and dive straight back into bed, acting as if nothing had happened.

Hidden safely behind the bushes, no-one ever saw their stash. Then, come next day, siesta time, they would stack the rest of their stolen goods, inside their jackets, or down the side of their trouser legs and walk straight out, as cool as two cucumbers, their shopping bags jammed pack with the pillowcase of loot.

Funnily enough, no-one ever saw them. For, it was Mam's ruling that her girls were free to come and go shopping. So, no-one bothered to give them the third degree.

A regular occurrence – almost every day between 1pm and 2pm, they would make their way down to the local outdoor market. In fact, they had built up such a canny 'system of social exchange,' that they were recognised by the market people as 'regulars.' So regular were they, that if a couple of days went by and Myra did not see them, she used to get worried.

"Where's Frankie and Jonnie?" she would ask.

"We don't know," the others would say, shaking their shoulders dismissively. Then, when she saw them racing down the mud track, her face would light up, beaming all over and she'd say, "here comes lion and foxy, from the 'Big Farm,' all dressed up in their best woollies.' And the others used to laugh themselves silly.

"We here. We here, Myra," Frankie would shout, as she approached.

"Well! Frankie, Jonnie. What have you got for me today?" Myra would tease, her eyes glistening with curiosity.

"Oh! Lots. Lots!" they would chuckle mischievously, as they emptied their stash on her table.

"You see! Look. Tea, sugar, marmalade, jam, toilet rolls, face flannels, combs, brooches. We got plennie, plennie fo' you today, Myra." Then, they would stand there, their faces beaming with joy and Myra could count out and mark the stolen goodies:

2 packets of tea	10d
2 lbs of sugar	12d
6 toilet rolls	12d
4 combs	6d
2 brooches	10d

"Here you are girls, 50d. How about that eh!" And they would laugh like two wild hyenas, grab the money quickly and run for their lives.

They would run, as fast as their legs could carry them, making their way to Woolworths or British Home Stores and once there, they would buy nice clothes (usually from the sales heap), and then they would buy toiletries, or other items for the inmates.

Yes, they were doing well, these two women, Frankie and Jonnie.

No matter what they wore, they always looked smart. And, looking at them, you would hardly tell they were mentally retarded; nuts; daft as a brush.

Myra did have her suspicions as to where these goods were coming from, but she never asked any questions. So benevolent was she.

She used to say to them, "haven't you done well today," and then give them a pittance for the goods. Then later, she would sell it for 4 times its value.

She was making a good trade, a good living, doing well for herself, so why should she bother to start digging up dirt. Myra O'Keefe was no fool. She didn't ask one single question.

Frankie and Jonnie were making their mark on the business world it seemed, but their 'entrepreneur charade' was serving another purpose too. For, whilst they were busy, stealing and selling goods, Trixie got a respite from their frequent torturing of her. As apart from their occasional theft of her toilet rolls from her pillowcase, they were too occupied to bother her much.

She was also attending Hope Day centre twice a week, so she escaped their beady eyes for at least two days a week. There, she learnt Makaton, played mat bowls and joined the music class, strumming away at her guitar, carrying with her in a pillowcase her 'glad-rags and sad-rags' – the only things she ever owned.

She was a happy woman indeed. But that was not to be for long. Something was about to happen soon, which would change all that.

CHAPTER NINETEEN

Mam had punished Trixie, sent her out in the cold to scrub steps, sure, but deep down in her heart, she had a soft spot for her. She liked her really.

She knew that Trixie was a kind and caring person, so she decided to give her a special chore. A job she'd earned just like the others; a job she knew Trixie would enjoy doing.

So one morning, she called Trixie into the office. "Trixie," Mam said, "would you bring in my tea this afternoon? And!" she added, "from now on that is your job. Would you do it every day from now on?"

Taken by surprise, Trixie almost jumped for joy. She loved laying that tray, watching the china cups rattle as she arranged them, seeing their enamel sparkle, almost dancing in the air when she carried the tray in. And now she will be able to do that chore, take in the tray of tea to Mam, regularly! 'Ho! What a privilege!'

Trixie was indeed a very happy woman. But behind the scene, Frankie and Jonnie had overheard Mam. Now, they were boiling, raging with anger and jealousy.

"Did you 'ear dat Jonnie?" Frankie barked, when they were alone together. "Trixie takin' Mam tea to 'er. Now she takin' over we favour too. Ah tole you she would! Ah tole you so!" she raged, stamping her feet like a deposed lion who was just about to lose its kill to its enemy.

Frankie was going crazy.

"We car'n 'ave dat. We car'n 'ave dat." Jonnie cut in.

"We got to do sometin'. We got to do sometin'," Frankie snapped, temper boiling, burning like the blast from a fierce furnace.

"Yeah, we got to, we got to!" Jonnie agreed, a wry look on her face.

"Yeah! And wat! Wat!" Frankie asserted, looking at Jonnie anxiously.

"We go steal 'er guitar and sell it."

"Ha, ha! Ha, ha!" Frankie laughed. "Dats no good. We got to do sometin' better.

Jonnie looked at her, eyes rolling from side to side, up and down – she was thinking, thinking... Then, all of a sudden she burst out laughing.

Someone passed by. They stopped laughing, but Jonnie still had that sinister look on her face and Frankie didn't have to quiz her anymore. She knew what she was thinking.

"Dat's it! A got it." Frankie beamed. "We go murder Trixie, dis time."

"Eeem... eem!"... Jonnie squeaked. And so, like the mafia, in quiet contemplation, the plan was devised and settled. A perfect mix, these two, each understanding the other perfectly.

That night, they didn't sleep much. They talked and talked, scheming, planning, and plotting, until the early hours of the morning. Then, when the plan was hatched, they went to sleep, ready and waiting for the perfect opportunity to carry it out.

But first thing's first. They had to steal Trixie's guitar, if only for a laugh. So they waited until she was asleep, sneaked into her room, ran off with her guitar and sold it in the market the next day. They got 50d for it and giggled like two young kids.

Next morning, when Trixie woke up, she found her guitar missing. She sobbed her heart out. That instrument had put so much life in her, made her happy and now they had taken it away from her! She cried and cried...

But Frankie and Jonnie already had an answer. When questioned, they told Mam that they saw a man running out of Mercy Farm with the guitar under his arm. "They were too scared to do anything," they asserted, a forlorn look on their faces and so Mam had to drop the subject.

The next day Mam had Mortise locks fitted in both the front and back doors of Mercy Farm and Frankie and Jonnie giggled unashamedly.

Now that their first task was safely accomplished, it was time to execute the murder plan.

"Trixie." Frankie called out to her in the kitchen one day. "We sorry you los' you guitar. We wan' to give you a treat," Frankie assured her.

"Yeah! A treat, a treat!" Jonnie appealed an innocent look on her face.

"We wan' to take you shoppin' wit us," Frankie continued.

"Yeah! Shoppin', shoppin'!" Jonnie chanted, agreeing with her best friend's gestures.

"We go buy you knickers and chocolate buttons," Frankie insisted.

"Yeah! Knickers, buttons," Jonnie was chanting, her high-pitched voice sounding as if she was in a church chorus.

It was the only way Jonnie knew how to speak, chant along after her friend Frankie. For, her retarded mind did not allow her to talk any differently. All she could do was talk in a squeaky voice in order to make herself understood.

When Trixie heard she was going out shopping to get a new pair of knickers, her eyes lit up. She always took pride in her clothes and now she was so happy. Mam, always encouraged it too. 'Shopping was a form of therapy," she assured her girls. And so the bait was set.

Trixie was ready to take the bait, poor mite – she just didn't know what was waiting for her.

Next morning, Frankie and Jonnie were up bright and early. And Trixie? Well she was dressed in her best outfit, her pink trouser suit, ready to go shopping.

"You ready Trix?"

"Ye-ah, ye-ah, ye-ah," Trixie went, her face ecstatic with joy.

"Come on den, let's go," they commanded, shoving her forward gently and slam! The front door shut tightly behind them.

They were away.

"Trix?" Frankie asserted, when they were safely outside the door, "We go walk troug de park girl. Watch de lake, feed de ducks, den we go to de shops."

"Ye-ah, ye-ah! Ye-ah, ye-ah!" Trixie agreed excitedly, anxious to get there and watch the ducks swimming. It was a long time since she'd been to the park and she was anxious to do anything. She was so excited.

With zest, they raced down to the park as fast as their legs could carry them and within minutes, they were there, standing beside the lake.

It was exactly 10am that Tuesday morning.

Jonnie looked around, her shifty eyes searching the place: straining, looking, zooming, as far as she could see. Behind bushes, shrubs, trees, flowers, anything her foxy eyes could see; like a panoramic lens, they zoomed in. But it was quiet; even the lake was still – not a ripple on its surface, nor a single duck floating. They had gone to roost, or so it seemed. It was so quiet, so still, so stone dead.

Then, all of a sudden, "Look! Trixie. Look! A fish!" Frankie shouted, pointing at something moving in the water.

"Ye-ah, Quick! Trixie, look!" Jonnie reinforced, Trixie rushed over to have a peep.

"Bend, Trixie. Bend! And you go see it better," Frankie was egging her on, Jonnie's eyes were zooming around the place to see if anyone was around. Then, as quick as a flash, as Trixie bent over, Frankie pushed her into the lake.

"A-ah...! A-ah...!" Trixie screamed. And, like a flash, a man darted from behind the bushes. He was standing there, watching his dog have a pee and he saw Frankie push Trixie over.

The still world was not so silent, after all.

Like lightening, he jumped into the lake, Trixie bobbing up and down now with her mouth opening and closing, as she gasped for air. Trixie O'Connor couldn't swim.

He grabbed her by the shoulders, lifted her face above the water, and swam and swam until he reached the water's edge? Frankie and Jonnie stood there scared out of their wits; frightened, not for Trixie, but of what this man might do to them.

There they stood, motionless, sweating.

Without ceremony, he laid Trixie on her tummy, pressed and released, pressed and released her ribcage, until, like a spring without a warning, water suddenly gushed from her mouth and slowly but surely she sprung to life. She was moving her limbs now and with the help of the man, managed to pull herself up. Then, for a moment she sat there, shaking, bewildered, frightened.

She started to cry.

"Now, which one of you pushed her in?" the man yelled.

Like two scared rabbits, Frankie and Jonnie were standing there, shivering.

"I said! Which one of you did it?" he barked.

He knew very well who did it, but he was going to squeeze it out of them, give them the fright of their lives, if he must.

Frankie and Jonnie were crying, whining like two hound dogs now and the man couldn't help.

"You come from the farm now, don't you? Mercy Farm, up there on the hill?"

"Ye-s. Yes…" they both stuttered, whimpering, whining and shaking like two withering leaves, trembling in the wind.

He stood there for a moment, half-musing, knowing very well that if they came from Mercy Farm they were bound to be retarded. So there was no point in pushing further.

"Right! Come on now!" he commanded. I'll take you there.

They stood there, frozen.

"Move! Move!" he shouted.

Trembling, they marched forward; Trixie, the man and his dog, following closely on their heels.

He was mad. He was angry. But he kept his calm, that is, until he reached Mercy Farm.

With a will of iron, he rang the doorbell.

"My name is Drummond. Frank Drummond! And I wish to see the Head of this Home."

"Certainly Sir, certainly!" the frightened carer acquiesced, almost bowing, but barely opening the door. She scampered down the corridor as fast as her legs could carry her, hardly even noticing Frankie, Jonnie and Trixie standing there behind the man.

She was back in a jiffy.

"Miss McCorkindale will see you Sir," she addressed him courteously, opening the door just enough to let him in.

As speedy as electricity, he charged in, Frankie, Jonnie, Trixie and the dog, following his trail – a distraught look on their faces – faces hiding a tale, which only they alone knew.

CHAPTER TWENTY

Frank Drummond barged straight into Miss McCorkindale's office, his clothes seeping wet, his face like thunder.

"My name is Drummond, Frank Drummond! And I have brought back three of your charges."

Taken aback, Miss McCorkindale looked at him, puzzled. She wasn't sure what reason he had to escort three of her girls back to their home, but she was prepared to listen. She braced herself, sat back on the chair and looking at him from above the rim of her spectacles, she cocked her ears listening, inquisitively.

"This woman, the big one!" (looking at Frankie hard) he continued, "pushed that one, the one with her tongue bobbing in and out of her mouth, straight into the lake. Coldwater Lake. But for me she would have drowned."

"What?"

Shocked at what she'd just heard, Miss McCorkindale went a little funny, her face turning red. But quickly, she pulled herself together again, sat bolt upright and continued to focus her steely gaze on Drummond, questioning… questioning… then, all of a sudden she shifted it onto Frankie and Frankie started to bawl.

"Ah did'n do it Mam! Ah did'n do it!" Frankie was pleading, crying like a soppy dog, a forlorn look on her face, scared and trembling, her fat knees almost knocking together, as she shook helplessly. Jonnie, meanwhile stood there, with a vacant expression on her face. It was the telltale sign and Mam knew that.

'She would deal with Frankie later,' Mam thought, 'when she'd finished with Frank Drummond.' So, without further adieu, she rang the bell and instructed that Frankie,

Jonnie and Trixie, be taken to the Day Room. "And!" she ordered, "change Trixie's clothing and stay there with them too." Susie the carer timidly marched away, her three charges following suit.

Trixie was shivering like a wet rabbit.

Turning to Drummond Miss McCorkindale said, "Please Sir, do continue."

She poured the cup of tea from the tray that Susie had brought in and Frank Drummond began to drink. As he drank, he told her everything.

"I took my dog for a walk in the park, Madam," he asserted, "and whilst he was having a pee, I saw the big woman push the other one into the lake…"

"Oh my God!" Miss McCorkindale went, as if she didn't believe him.

"Yes Madam, it is true," he continued, babbling on and on. Miss McCorkindale listened with fear in her eyes, shocked to the bone, his frightening tale only to be interrupted by the intermittent barking of his dog.

"Hush, Bimbo. Hush!" he commanded the poor whining creature went all quiet again, and sprawled out on his belly.

"I could see her drowning," Drummond continued, "so I rushed over, dived in, pulled her to the water's edge and squeezed the water out of her lungs.

"God help us!" Miss McCorkindale went.

"But for me," Drummond concluded, "she would have died."

"God save us all!" Miss McCorkindale cried, the blood slowly returning to her ashen face.

She didn't want to hear how he'd pumped the water out of Trixie's lungs. She'd heard enough and she didn't wish to hear him rambling on again. So she poured another cup of tea for him.

She couldn't believe Frankie could do such a thing. Frankie, in whom she had placed her trust; Frankie, who she had given so many privileges to. She, Frankie, had tried to murder Trixie?

She couldn't believe it! But then, Frankie was a half-witted woman, mentally retarded and somehow, Mam, so keen on trying to give her girls a normal life, overlooked that fact. Now, she had a catastrophe on her hands and she knew she had to deal with it quickly.

She thanked Mr Drummond for his kind deed and he left sharply, feeling quite disturbed by the whole incident.

He could see that Miss McCorkindale was a stern woman. 'She would handle it,' he hoped, but somewhere deep inside he had a funny feeling that she didn't believe him. He wasn't sure whether he should inform the police or not.

His mind going adrift, he made his way slowly down the hill, his dog Bimbo following swiftly at his heels.

As soon as he left her office, Miss McCorkindale rang the bell.

"Bring Frankie in!" she commanded, her face like thunder.

"Frankie!" she barked. Frankie was shaking nervously, her knees almost rattling. "You pushed Trixie into the lake. Didn't you? Mr Drummond saw you doing it."

"No! No! No!" Frankie howled, pleading like a fat, puppy dog.

"Frankie, I could call the police and have them arrest you for attempted murder," Mam's eyes were fixed – as cold as steel.

"Oh God. No! No!…" Frankie screamed, weeping like a child. She was, pleading, pleading, begging…

Mam, looked at her as if she was the devil himself.

She had no intention of calling the police. For, she knew if she did that, the authorities might close down Mercy Farm and she had no intention of letting that happen or giving her home a bad reputation. She would deal with it in her own way; give Frankie the fright of her life, if only to teach her a lesson.

Frankie stood there bawling her head off, looking like a bewildered sheep and Mam felt sorry for her.

'Such a pitiful sight,' she thought. But she knew she had to teach her that lesson.

"Alright! Alright! Frankie," Mam barked. "But!… you must be punished! Frankie, punished! We can't have you going around trying to kill people now, can we?" Mam, asserted angrily, pointing her finger straight at Frankie's nose, Frankie, not knowing what she might do next.

"Punished! Frankie, punished! Understood! Frankie, understood!"

Big Frankie was shaking so much, she almost went into convulsions.

"Now!" Mam continued, "I want you to go to the bottom of the landing, with a brush, soap and bucket of water and scrub the corridor dry. Scrub… scrub… that corridor until you can see your face in it. Understood! Frankie. Understood!" she roared, her horn-rimmed spectacles almost cracking. Then, like a mad woman, she banged the bell hard and without ceremony, Frankie was escorted by Susie to begin her laborious task of scrubbing the stone corridor.

Frankie was 42, mentally retarded and so had a child-like mind – that's why she tried to kill Trixie, as a child would. But Mam, had a home to run and so dealt with it in the only way she knew how. 'Reward, punishment. correction' – that was her method.

She had meted out the same punishment as she did Trixie, not because she was a stickler for punishment, but because she was trained that way – Behaviour Modification was her method. It was what she believed.

'The best way to maintain social order,' she thought, 'was correction. Hold up Frankie's sins to her; let her see the error of her ways. Only then could she make conscious efforts to correct them.'

Yes, Mam firmly believed in that theory of Behaviourism – correction, was the name of the game.

And so, Frankie was sent on her mission to scrub steps, in the hope that she would correct her sins.

She scrubbed and scrubbed for hours on end. Scrubbing that cold stone corridor, her broad back aching, her fat legs wobbling, her skirt seeping in soap suds and the staff taking the 'Mick' out of her.

"Hurry up Frankie," they taunted, as they passed by. "Hurry up old girl, or Father Christmas may pass you by and you won't get your present this time."

They tortured her as she sobbed her heart out, as Trixie did, scrubbing... scrubbing... scrubbing... out in the cold, for 5 solid hours while Jonnie, lay low indoors, scared as a rabbit.

Frankie and Jonnie had learnt to play the game well, only this time the game was played against them.

CHAPTER TWENTY-ONE

Frank Drummond arrived home that day, a very disturbed man. The clothes on his body were almost dry by then, but there was something on his mind bothering him. He was in a predicament. He was not very happy and he went very quiet.

Ettie, his wife, could sense that something was wrong; the way he went all quiet, shutting himself off from her and she didn't like what she was seeing.

That evening, they had their usual supper: cottage pie, jam roly-poly topped with custard and a nice hot pot of tea. But Frank Drummond sat quietly throughout the whole supper. He hardly said a word.

It was unusual for Frank to be so quiet, for he was the one who did most of the talking. And though Ettie tried to break the ice, strike up a conversation, all she got from him was a straight 'yes' or 'no.' Not a single word more. She couldn't bear it. She'd reached the point where she could take no more.

"Come on now Frank. What's up?" she enquired. "You have never been one to keep quiet at the table!"

Frank shrugged his shoulders. "It's nothing, nothing!" he barked and continued to pick at his food.

"Come on now Frank," she coaxed. "Ah know somethin's wrong. Look at you, all bottled up inside and you don't look well, too!"

Frank knew what was bothering him, but he didn't want to tell Ettie. It was not so much the incident at Coldwater Lake that was getting to his skin, but what the police might do to him if he did report the crime.

That's what was getting him down and there was no way he could tell Ettie.

"Look Frank," Ettie insisted, putting down her cup of tea on the table. "Ah don't like the looks of you. And to be honest Frank, a don't think ah can take no more of this hiding things from me; you shutting yourself from me, knowing that somethin's wrong and you don't bother to tell me. How do you think I feel?"

"Look at you Frank. Look at you!"

Frank bent his head and thought for a minute. He didn't like upsetting Ettie. He knew she was right, but he just didn't know how to tell her. He just wasn't sure how she would take it. Frank Drummond was in limbo.

"I am your wife, Frank," Ettie appealed. "For forty years now we've been together and if somethin's botherin' you, don't you think I should know? It pains me as much as it hurts you, Frank. You know that!"

Frank looked at Ettie with pain in his heart. All his life, he'd loved this woman and now she was hurting so much. He suddenly felt as if a sharp pin had just pricked him in his heart and knew that he could keep his suffering from her no more. She was right – he knew that. Come what may, he must brace himself and tell her everything, from beginning to end.

"Ettie!" he said. "It was terrible! Ettie, terrible!"

"Terrible! What do you mean, Frank?" What do you mean?"

"Well, you see, it's like this Ettie. I took Bimbo for a walk in the park and whilst he was peeing, I saw a woman push another one in the Lake. You could imagine how I felt Ett… I just couldn't stand and watch the woman drowning. So, I rushed over, pulled her out of the water, squeezed the water out of her lungs and by some miracle, I managed to save the woman's life. It was a miracle Ett… a miracle.

For a moment, Ettie looked at him, shocked. Then, she quickly pulled herself together and…

"And!… what woman was this, Frank? The one who pushed the other?" she enquired, the shock telling in her eyes.

"Do you know who this woman was?"

"Yes Ett... yes. A woman from Mercy Farm. After I rescued this woman, I took them down to Mercy Farm and the Head told me so. Frankie, she was called, Ett... Frankie. Big, she was, 18 stones or so. She could have killed the other one Ett... she could have killed her."

"You mean them weirdos from that big house up there on the hill?" Ettie continued.

"Right! Ett... right. Spot on! Ett... Spot on!"

"But you went to the Head, that strange woman and you reported it to the police, of course?"

"No Ett... No! That's just it, you see. I dare not go to the police because I am afraid what they might do to me."

"What do you mean Frank? What do you mean?"

"Because Ett... I witnessed the crime. And because them women are loonies, the police may think I did it."

"But they can't Frank, they can't. You are telling the truth and they will believe you."

Frank knew Ettie was right. The police may not believe him. They may even put him in jail for attempted murder. But he had to take that chance. He had to report the crime. He couldn't walk around with that on his conscience.

For a moment, his mind went adrift again, remembering too well, how, a few years back, one of the women from Mercy Farm had drowned in that same lake. Rumours had it that it was murder; that one of the women had killed the other. And though the police were not involved and it was not in the papers, it was amazing how gossip spread.

No one was able to ascertain whether it was fact or fiction, but like wild-fire, it spread. Hot gossip. Women standing around, talking about, 'those loonie women from Mercy Farm. How those weirdos were fighting and killing each other. And one of them,' the rumour went, 'was found dead, floating on the lake.'

'Murder! It was. Murder!'

'And many a person saw her ghost, much later on – a mermaid she was. Half woman, half fish, sitting at the edge of the lake, combing her long dark hair.'

109

Hot gossip abounded about that body in the lake; facts that were never proven, but the gossip continued to circulate, nonetheless.

Frank could not cope with his drifting mind, so he went up to bed to have a rest.

That evening, whilst they were having their hot chocolate together, Frank looked at Ettie with a distraught look in his eyes. He lowered his head. He was thinking, scared, frightened of what the police might do to him. He didn't want to go to the police station and Ettie could almost read his mind.

"It's no good Frank. It's no good. You've got to go to the police. You know that."

Sitting gingerly on his chair near the fire, Frank scratched his head and rubbed his chin, but did not say a single word. Instead, he went off to bed, quietly, pondering about the predicament he'd found himself in.

Next morning, he was up bright and early. He made a tray of tea and took it up to Ettie.

"You know what love? You are right," he declared. "I am going down to the police station today to report the whole matter.

Ettie felt so relieved, she gave him a great big hug, kissed him smack, straight on the lips and made him blush.

He sat on the edge of the bed and together they drank the tea. They talked and talked a lot about what he would say and what he wouldn't when he got to the police station. The matter was now well and truly settled.

That morning, they finished their breakfast downstairs as usual. Then, as if to reassure himself, Frank Drummond hugged Ettie tightly, squeezed her a little, and then made swiftly for the front door.

He flattened his felt cap on his head, put on his brown, worn out coat and made his way briskly to Mountjoy Police Station.

CHAPTER TWENTY-TWO

As he made his way there, he could see Mountjoy Police Station, standing all alone, built high up on a flattened mound of massive concrete, so that it could take the weight of the mighty Mountjoy.

In the cellars below, prisoners were held, waiting anxiously for a few days or so, waiting indefinitely for news of their cases; waiting forever it seemed. Small cells in which you could hardly swing a cat; bare dirty walls, graffiti-laden; a hard, thin mattress on the floor; a dirty toilet pan in the far corner that never saw the light of soap or a scrubbing brush. It stank to high heaven.

Nervously, Frank hurried up the steps and pushed the swing-door open. No one was at the desk. He was just about to ring the bell when, as if from nowhere, a policeman appeared.

"Can I help you Sir?" the Officer enquired, his fat belly wobbling above the belt of his dark trousers with the distinctive silver-black cap perched firmly on his head.

"Yes…?" Drummond replied. He was nervous. He was hesitant and the Officer could sense this.

"So! What can I do for you Sir?" the Officer asked again.

"Well, you see Officer…" Drummond tried to brace himself, but he was sweating away at the palms now. He was shaking; frightened in case they decided to lock him in the cell, as the perpetrator of the crime he was just about to report. He was sweating.

"O'Mally! Jerry O'Mally!" the policeman intercepted. Officer Jerry," he asserted, as he watched Frank sweat away.

"Well you see Officer Jerry… I have just witnessed… an attempted murder."

"Attempted murder, eh! Ha… Ha!… Ha… ha!…" Officer Jerry laughed, taking out a bent cigarette from his dirty jacket pocket and lighting it.

"You got to believe me," Drummond insisted, going red in the face. "I have just seen a…"

"Wey, Wey! Hold on now. Hold on! First things first! Now, may I have your name and address Sir?"

"My name is Drummond! Frank Drummond! And I live at 10 Coldwater Drive."

"Good! Now, good! So Frank, now tell me what exactly did you see?"

"As I was about to say Officer, I was taking my dog Bimbo for a walk in the park and whilst Bimbo was having a pee, I saw a big woman push another small woman in the lake."

"In the lake eh. And which lake?"

"Coldwater."

"Coldwater Lake eh. Ha…Ha!… Ha… Ha!… Jerry laughed again, his shoulders heaving, his wide jaw about to crack, showing his dirty, yellow, nicotine-stained teeth. He was laughing so loud, his mate Jack heard the ruction and came out to investigate.

"It's alright Jack! It's OK! Frank saw a woman from Mercy Farm trying to drown another one in the lake."

Jack looked at Frank, smiled, and then disappeared again.

"Now, Frank. Tell me more," Jerry was enticing Frank. He couldn't keep his face straight.

"Like I was saying, Officer Jerry, this big woman Frankie, pushed the other one, Trixie, into the lake. I could see her drowning, so I rushed over, jumped straight in and swam and swam, carrying Trixie to the edge of the water. And…" he paused, Jerry showing a little more interest now, jotted down notes, haphazardly.

"And!... Go on Frank! Go on! Tell me more!" he coaxed, his burnt out cigarette lying on the ashtray, dead.

"And!..." Frank continued. He was shaking like a leaf now. "I turned Trixie over on her stomach, squeezed the water out of her lungs and she came to life again."

"Well! Well! Well! You do surprise me Frank," Jerry went, trying hard to keep his face straight. He lit up another cigarette and took a drag from it. "So," he continued interrogating Frank who was getting the gibbers now.

"So it's like this... You witnessed a woman from Mercy Farm attempting to drown another one. You dived in and saved her life."

"Mercy Farm eh! Where them weirdoes live?" He howled, almost doubling up in his swivel chair.

He didn't like Frank Drummond. 'The way that man looked; didn't seem to have his balls about him; dry, guilty eyes and that funny felt cap on his head!' He didn't believe him.

'Gentleman Frank! Never!'

Jerry O'Mally could tell a liar when he spotted one. And Frank Drummond was certainly one. 'He probably heard rumours about the woman from Mercy Farm who once drowned in that lake and now he cooked up a perfect story to gain glory, no doubt.' Jerry O'Mally shook his head.

He lit another cigarette, puffed and blew smoke straight above his head. "So you are saying Frank, a woman from Mercy Farm tried to drown another one. Them loonies, nutters? Ha... Ha!... Ha!..." Jerry laughed, almost going into convulsions now.

Jerry O'Mally did not believe Frank Drummond. 'Those weirdo women just did not have the brains to plan such a murder' he thought. 'They just didn't have the sense.' But he would go along with Frank, if only for appearance sake.

"Ha... Ha!... Ha... Ha!..." he laughed again, "is that all Frank?"

"Yes Mr O'Mally, that's all."

"Sign here please."

Poor Frank. He was telling the truth and no-one believed him.

Frank Drummond signed the Statement with relief; relieved that Jerry O'Mally didn't lock him away.

"Thank God," he said to himself, quietly, as he walked away. "Many an innocent bastard ended up in that jailhouse through no fault of their own. Thank God," he whispered again, as he made his way swiftly from Mountjoy Police Station, wishing that he had never gone there in the first place.

CHAPTER TWENTY-THREE

It was 10am on Monday morning, when Sergeant Jerry O'Mally drove down to Mercy Farm to investigate the incident. He had sensitive business to do, so he decided to drive there quietly and do it all alone. He didn't switch his siren on. Nor did he flash his lights.

Placing his finger firmly on the doorbell, his eyes wandered around the grounds of the building, searching for some clue that may help his decision. Then, someone opened the door. It was Susie, the carer.

Shocked, to see this big, burly policeman standing on the doorstep, her eyes widened, wondering what he was doing there and she felt a little queasy. She was shaking at the knees now, but then she quickly pulled herself together again.

"Yes Officer?" she enquired hesitantly. "Can I help you?"

"Jerry O'Mally. Jerry O'Mally, my love, the Sergeant from Mountjoy," he declared in a firm but friendly manner. "I would like to see the Head of the Home if you don't mind, Miss?"

Susie was getting the jitters now. She never did like the police, ever since her dad was imprisoned wrongfully some time ago, for something he didn't do. 'And now this one – this Sergeant, what do you call him? – is here to see Miss McCorkindale.' She didn't like that.

She knew there was a barney between Frankie and Trixie, but she didn't think it was anything serious. 'Just horsing around, they were.' Everyone thought that.

She looked at the Sergeant, her eyes widening with fear, then, "Sure, Sure!" she blurted. "Come in Sir. Come in! And, please wait here, while I go and find Miss McCorkindale," she added.

She hurried down the corridor, leaving him standing in the entrance, his eyes sussing out the place. He looked at the two photos of the inmates hanging on the wall and he felt a little sad. But then, Susie returned and disturbed his thoughts.

"Miss McCorkindale will see you now, Sir," she interrupted and led him straight to the office; he marching along behind her, cap in hand.

Sitting firmly behind her desk, Miss McCorkindale waved him in. "Do come in Sir, Sit! Sit!" she commanded. He moved swiftly into the office, but remained standing.

"Jerry O'Mally, Mam, Sergeant Jerry O'Mally from Mountjoy Police Station!" he greeted, stretching his hand out to shake hers, but she barely touched it.

"Yes Mr O'Mally, I guessed who you were," she replied stiffly, not budging from behind her desk.

"Mam," he continued searchingly, "I guess you know why I am here."

"No! Mr O'Mally. No! I do not know, Sergeant, and I do not guess anything."

She had an inclination, but she wasn't going to let on now. She was going to fight to keep her home clean. Play the boxing match, if she had to and she wasn't going to give in now.

Sergeant O'Mally shifted his feet and coughed a little.

"Mam," he continued, "I am sorry to have to break the news like this, but a man called Frank Drummond, made a complaint against one of your girls."

"What! A complaint! A man called Drummond? Surely..." she shook her head. "My girls are decent girls, Sergeant. I've taught them to live clean, Mr O'Mally, and I am staggered to hear this." She fixed her fiery eyes firmly on O'Mally now.

"Mam," O'Mally proceeded, trying to take control. "Mr Drummond came down to Mountjoy on Friday and made this complaint."

"A complaint! What complaint? Mr O'Mally. Do tell me."

"Mr Drummond said, Mam, that one your girls, a big one called Frankie, pushed another one, named Trixie, straight into Coldwater Lake and she nearly drowned."

"Murder! Sergeant O'Mally. Attempted Murder! Is that what you saying, Sir?" her chestnut eyes ablaze now.

"No Mam. Not exactly Mam, it's just…" Sergeant O'Mally was losing ground and he wasn't very happy.

"It's just what Sergeant?" Miss McCorkindale interrupted. "My girls are clean living girls. How could anyone say such a vile thing about them? That is ridiculous Sergeant. And you know it."

Miss McCorkindale was almost jumping for joy, for she knew that she was gaining ground.

For a moment, Sergeant O'Mally stood there, still. He was used to taking command, but now he was losing his grip. When he'd first arrived, she'd offered him a seat, but he preferred to stand, for he felt better able to take charge, take command, standing. Now, somehow, he'd lost his bite.

Mam, meanwhile, was determined to make her stand. She had a reputation for being the 'Iron Lady' and so, pitted against her, O'Mally had almost lost his bearing.

"Mr Drummond said, Mam," he continued, "that he jumped into the lake and saved Trixie."

"Saved Trixie? Ha! Bravo to him!" she laughed sarcastically, leaving O'Mally feeling disturbed.

He shifted his leg again, but determined to continue, he proceeded, "And Mam, I was a little concerned about his story, because…" He didn't finish his sentence.

"Good for you, Sergeant! Good for you! How could anyone believe such a thing about my girls? My Angels." She banged the bell hard and summoned Trixie to the office.

Jerry O'Mally could not tell Miss McCorkindale why he was concerned about Drummond's evidence. That would be 'a breach of confidence' and would most certainly ruin his career, so he tried to go along with her, if only for appearance sake.

Trixie appeared, shaking.

"Trixie?" Mam coaxed. "Did Frankie push you into the lake?"

"Na-ah… Ha-ah! Na-ah… Na-ah!" Trixie cried, tongue bobbing in her mouth, the Sergeant looking on with pity in his eyes. She knew that Frankie had done it, but she didn't want to cause any trouble. For, that was the type of person she was.

"There! You see Sergeant O'Mally? There's your evidence, right here, in front of your nose," Mam intervened. "Frankie did not push Trixie into that lake! And you know it."

Sergeant O'Mally scratched his head. He knew he couldn't accept Trixie's evidence. She was mentally retarded and even if she did say anything, her words would not stand up in a Court of Law. And Miss McCorkindale knew that too, but she had to make a stand, show her strength if she must; each playing the game, set and match, against the other.

Mam suspected that Frankie had done it, but she didn't give a damn. What she was most concerned about, was the reputation of her home. She didn't want to lose her license. She was making a good living and she didn't want to lose that.

Jerry O'Mally knew he didn't have a case. He couldn't arrest a mentally retarded woman for 'Attempted Murder.' That would never stand up and think of the uproar it would cause!

To tarnish that home with such a reputation! Think what it would do to it and to society as a whole. It could be the end of him. Ruin him for good.

He had just one more year to go before he retired and he was not going to rock this boat, nor any other one, for that matter.

He scratched his chin. Only this time, he didn't look at Mam.

"Well? OK, Mam! Ok! There's no need for Trixie to give evidence. Both the girls were horsing around, weren't they? Playing games with each other, anyway. And that's how it was. That! Mam! Is the end of the matter."

He didn't even stop to look at her face.

Bowing slightly as he left, Sergeant Jerry O'Mally, the liberal policeman, made his way out of Mercy Farm, jumped into his car and drove swiftly to Mountjoy Police Station, without pressing any charges.

For now, at least, Miss McCorkindale would continue to make a good living.

CHAPTER TWENTY-FOUR

Time moved on and things were ticking over slowly at Mercy Farm, when something happened which was to change all that. Miss McCorkindale died.

She was driving home from a business meeting, one bleak winter's evening in January 1987, thinking about the day's event. She had a lot on her mind and was thinking hard, when she was hit by a truck and so met her sudden and tragic death.

It was pitch black that evening and even with the headlights on, you couldn't see a thing.

The cold wind charged at 70 miles an hour, howling, blustering, snow flakes drifting everywhere, when suddenly, in the darkness, as if from nowhere, a huge lorry appeared and 'bang!' It crashed straight into Mam's little Morris Minor ramming it head on, into the bonnet of her car and smashing it to pieces.

She died instantly. Her body crushed, blood everywhere; her face so badly disfigured that it was beyond recognition.

A tragic disaster, it was indeed! And now it was left to Mam's staff to break the sad news to her 15 inmates. Heart-breaking, sad and gruelling as it was, they had to do it, and so they tried to do it as gently as they could. They waited for the right moment.

Keeping a low profile, teatime came and they decided it was time to break the news, as easily as they could.

"Mam is dead," the two carers said. "She died suddenly from a car crash," they added, tentatively.

It went quiet. There was such a hush that you could hardly hear a pin drop. All but two went into a state of shock

– the carers moving around, in between, hugging and trying to comfort them, with sad expressions on their faces.

Frankie and Jonnie didn't bat an eyelid. Blank expressions on their faces, they didn't show any feelings or pain. They just took it in their stride.

They knew they had each other and come what may, they would survive. And so they clung together so much, that rumours went around that they were lesbians, even though no one could prove it. They simply fed, one off the other, and that's how they survived.

For Trixie O'Connor though, it was a different story. She was sad. She was distraught. She was in a state of shock.

She knew Mam had a soft spot for her and she had even grown to like Mam. She used to love taking in that tray of tea to her. 'And now she was dead!' she couldn't believe it. She just couldn't take it. She burst into tears.

She went outside, sat on the cold bench and sobbed her heart out. She was bawling so much, sobbing, sobbing, the icy wind biting into her unsuitably-clad body and no-one could shift her.

Seeing her shivering in the cold, Josie went out. "Come on Trixie," she coaxed, putting a coat around her shoulders, but Trixie wouldn't budge. "Come on girl," she badgered, putting her arms around her shoulders, but Trixie did not move.

"Look Trix… Look! We've made a nice hot cup of chocolate for you, and your favourite vanilla cake too!" Carmen called from inside the building, trying to entice her in, but to no avail.

She wouldn't even look at them. She just sat there and cried and cried and cried…

They got worried, so, in desperation they took the hot chocolate and cake out there to her, but she didn't even touch it. It just laid there on the bench, stone cold.

She grieved and cried for three solid hours and only came inside when it started to bucket down with rain.

That night, she got a chill. She shivered and sweated, her body temperature rising, Josephine applying cold compresses to her forehead, feeding her with hot drinks, but still she kept on shivering. She hardly slept a wink.

Next morning, they got so concerned, they called the doctor in. When he examined her he found she had caught pneumonia. He prescribed antibiotics and left instructions for them to phone him if her condition worsened.

During the night, Josephine pumped antibiotics and drinks down into her and wrapped her in extra blankets, so that she could sweat the fever out. Eventually, she fell asleep and began to dream…

She dreamt: 'She was visited by a Prince who took her away in his golden chariot – somewhere – she didn't know where. Only, this place was like a palace!

Romantic renaissance paintings: Monet, Rembrandt, Goya, in gold, gilded frames, adorned the walls. Exotic embroidered tapestries hung in front of huge fireplaces. Silver candelabras standing there like sentinels on long polished tables, sprucely laid out with Royal Albert and Worcester porcelain. And silver cutlery, polished to a sheen, ready, as if in waiting for the guests to arrive.'

Magnificent, they were, such beautiful things; things she would never in her real life see. 'Exotic Oriental and Frisian rugs covered the floor. Ceilings with Raphaelite paintings – paintings of angels carrying flutes, dancing up there, forming patterns high up in the air.'

The truth is, Trixie O'Connor did not know the names of these paintings. Her retarded mind was not versed in art and could not retain such intricacies, such pompous details. All she knew was, it was like being in heaven. It was magic! Her dream told her so.

She was still sweating and in her half-dazed mind, she could see the Prince, 'dressed in his blue and gold-edged tunic, beckoning her on… handing her something…

She wasn't sure what it was, but, as she reached out to take it, wearing her exquisite pale-blue silk gown,' she woke up... suddenly.

Like an intruder who had just been confronted by an inmate, she was startled. She jumped... scared... She was sweating; hot sweat pouring from her, like beads on a string.

Looking around her now, she was quickly brought to reality. All she could see was the bare whitewashed walls of her room and flakes falling from its ceiling. She was scared, lost and frightened.

"It's alright! It's alright!" Josephine the night carer whispered. "You just had a dream, that's all. You were whispering something... something... about a Prince I think."

She looked around her, hot, half-dizzy, half-dazed, not quite sure where she was, or what was happening, but with repeated coaxing and re-assurance from Josephine, she soon fell asleep again.

For several days after, they pumped antibiotics and drinks down her. Then, after a week or so, she recovered and slowly returned to her usual self again. But then, that dream haunted her, or what she could remember of it.

'A Prince! With gifts and a golden chariot! What a dream! Me with a Prince! Never!...'

She shrugged her shoulders and tried to dismiss it. But then, reality was to hit her straight in the face; the reality – the fact that Mam was dead.

For twenty years, Mam had run that strange home, Mercy Farm, with a strictness and dedication that was hard to match. She never did manage to get married or have children. With 15 inmates to look after, she didn't need kids. Besides, at £250 per week, per head, she had quickly become a millionairess and she was indeed a very happy woman.

But now that she was dead, there was no-one to leave her millions to. The State would have it all and the 'girls' as she called her inmates, would have to move on – find a new place in which to live.

Susannah Denton, would see to it. That was her job.

123

For 17 years, Trixie had lived at Mam's home, Mercy Farm. She had grown accustomed to that home; grown to like it. And now at 42, she would be moving yet again, shuntered around from place to place, carrying with her, a worn-out pillowcase containing her glad-rags and sad-rags, the only things she ever possessed in the whole wild world.

Trixie O'Connor started to cry, a deep howling wail, coming low down from inside her stomach.

CHAPTER TWENTY-FIVE

Times had changed and things were changing fast.

Now in 1987, Susannah Denton was no longer a Social Visitor. Now, she was a Qualified Social Worker, well versed in social work theories: Group Therapy, Family Therapy; you name it, she had it rehearsed – 'modern concepts,' they were called. Only, most of her clients did not have families on which to practise her theories.

And the County Council was paying her anything up to £500 a week for that! It was hard to believe.

The Peabody Organisation had also changed – it was changing all the time. For, as new Acts and Policies came into force in Britain, it too had changed.

To begin with, following the 1971 Education Act, the Society started placing more emphasis on Day Care Training. 'Assisted Learning' – they called it, and appropriately, it changed its name to the Peabody Centre.

Trixie used to attend there twice a week, from Mercy Farm. She started learning Makaton, joined other classes and was learning to bake cakes too.

But then, by 1987, when Miss McCorkindale died, the Centre had undergone far-reaching changes. For, in line with the 1981 Education Act, every learning disabled person in care, had to undergo Annual Reviews, so that they would be given the support and resources to meet their individual needs.

Yes, the Society was moving with the times, or so they thought.

But every new Act and Policy was costing the nation money.

At least six people had to attend these Reviews: The Home's Manager, Key Worker, Placement Officer, Instructor, Social Services Representatives and the Client herself. They had to formulate reports and each of them had to be paid for their services. And half the time, these professionals never bothered to turn up for the meetings. This was costing the taxpayer and the nation as a whole, money. But no-one bothered to count the cost.

Indeed, it was whilst returning from such a Review, that fatal evening, that Miss McCorkindale got killed in a car crash. She hated those Reviews. She used to go mad about them, 'waste of time and resources,' she would say. But still, no-one heard her cry. And no-one bothered to help her change things.

Many a person was making a good living for themselves; therefore, they were not going to rock the boat.

Jane Peabody's Charitable Enterprise was changing radically and there was not a damned thing they could do about it.

It was changing in line with current thinking and national policies, they claimed and so it changed its name to fit its current stance. Now in the 1980's, it was renamed Hope Centre, for it offered hope in the form of a two-pronged service: Day Care and Home Care for people with 'learning disabilities,' the new name given to mentally retarded people.

Its literature now reflected Social work jargon. It's aims were, it asserted: 'to promote the interests of people with Learning Disabilities; to allow them individual rights, choices, potential; to support each individual to develop their skills, interests, confidence, self-esteem and so enhance their place in the community'… Words, which the ordinary person could hardly make sense of; words dressed up in jargon, meaningless and faceless as the people who tried to put them into practice.

They, the so-called professionals, were deciding the fate: the rights, the wrongs and choices of people with learning disabilities – ordinary people who just wanted to be left alone to live simple lives.

As far as Trixie was concerned, she was certainly never given any choices. From the word go, she was snatched from her poor but caring parents, shunted from place to place, robbed of the chance of building a stable life. And even when she showed caring potential, those qualities were never allowed to develop.

She was never trained, helped or encouraged to take her place in society, as a carer would. The label of being 'mentally retarded' stuck with her. And even though they'd changed the name to 'learning disabilities' it made no difference to her life.

Trixie O'Connor would have made a good carer. With a little supervision, she could have claimed her place in the community in which she lived. But she was never given that chance. Instead, they, the professionals, squashed her desires, trampled on her rights, her ability to become a person in her own right.

It all started with her doctor really, who, when she was 18 months old (a mere toddler) examined her and decided that, under Section 1 of the Mental Defective Act 1913 to 1938, she was a 'defective', an 'imbecile'.

He based his conclusion on the grounds that she had the characteristics of a Mongol; oblique eyes; fissured tongue; attached earlobes and she was dirty, wet most of the time and had to be spoon fed.

It was hard to believe that a doctor, a medically qualified practitioner, had made such a decision. What does he expect from an 18 month old baby? She was a Mongol alright, but, surely there was room for development, improvement as she grew older? But this doctor didn't see it that way. He didn't give her that chance. Instead, he labelled her a 'defective' and she was treated as such for the rest of her life.

That label followed her wherever she went.

The 1983 Mental Health Act clearly defines a 'defective' as: 'a person who has severe impairment of intelligence and social functioning.'

But as Trixie grew older, she failed to display any of these two signs. Instead, she was sensitive, a great social mixer, loved camaraderie and enjoyed caring and sharing things.

When she was 40, her key worker wrote: 'Generous and readily shares sweets and goodies; last year, made great leaps forward; great team spirit, competitive but understands the rules of the game and plays accordingly; makes some sort of cakes and knows the order of ingredients; enjoys music and singing and uses hand-shapes well; speech improving.'

It is clear that these reports do not suggest 'severe impairment of intelligence and social functioning,' the recognised traits of a defective. Yet the doctor categorised her as such so she carried that stigma and remained in that 'box' for the rest of her days.

That label followed her everywhere. Even, the revamped Hope Centre didn't use their influence to rectify it, in spite of their observations on her.

The Centre was certainly changing alright, but only in so far as the authority dictated it should.

Now in the 1980s, Hope Centre had become an expensive commodity. It was employing highly paid staff: Social Workers at £500 or so a week; instructors at £5 an hour, mostly paid for by the County Council, via the nation's Social Services Department. And there were art teachers and therapist fees to be paid too.

On top of that, the Centre was charging anything between £70 and £90 per adult, per week, to attend its Day Care Unit, all paid for by the State. And 80 pence per person, per week, had to be forked out to pay for their transport.

For Residential Care or 'Family Homes', as they preferred to call it, home owners were paid anything between £265 to £400 a week, to care for each inmate. Only, these were not homes, but institutions. And inmates were lucky if they got their £14 a week pocket money entitlement, as this was used by the institutions to buy clothes and sundries for their clients.

Though, the charitable Peabody Organisation had become Hope Centre, an expensive enterprise, it was still seen by many as a charitable organisation. But it had become in part, a private company, funded partly, by lottery, grants, legacies and fundraising events, but in the main, from the nation's Social Services Department – in other words, the taxpayer's pocket.

In short, the taxpayer was paying for people like Trixie to be snatched from her home and family life and put in care in private institutions, camouflaged as family homes.

The philanthropist, Jane Peabody's dream was certainly shattered.

The vision she once had, of taking mentally retarded people out of institutions and placing them with real families was finished. Now, her Society was placing them back into institutions – the very thing she tried to avoid – institutions, housing anything up to 20 residents. The only difference being, they were disguised as family homes.

Now, the State was employing people with mind-blowing titles; titles like Key Workers, Placement Officers and so forth, paying them exorbitant wages for services which they really did not need. So, far from allowing these clients to exercise their independence, their rights and choices, they were becoming dependent on their charges – the institution and the State – for their very survival.

The institution had once again triumphed and somewhere along the line, Jane Peabody's vision was lost.

Just think! The nation, through its Social Services Department, was paying £500 or so a week, to keep Trixie in institutional care. If only they had given Trixie's mother, Betty O'Connor, one fifth of that £500 to care for her daughter Trixie, she would have remained with her parents and shared the warmth and love of her real family and their lives; a life that was hers by right. But they, the Social Services had taken away that right from her.

Instead, they forked out exorbitant sums to private institutions, enabling them to get rich and send their children to private schools, whilst she, Betty O'Connor, was left to die of poverty, her retarded daughter Trixie, shunted from place to place, robbed of family love and the stability of family life, which should have been hers by right.

And they were allowing clients to exercise their rights, or so they claimed. How times had changed!

Jane Peabody once had a dream. Now that dream had been turned on its head.

If only she knew, she would turn in her grave!

CHAPTER TWENTY-SIX

Henry Brockenhurst, was a man with a vision. As Managing Director of Hope Centre, he had great plans and high hopes for his protégés. 'Each was an individual in their own right,' he felt, 'who could be taught and trained to take up their rightful place in society.' But Henry couldn't see what many outsiders saw: a bunch of crackpots, lunatics, nutters, screwballs...

Henry Brockenhurst, didn't have a crystal ball.

Jennifer O'Brien, stood outside 8 Brimstone Way, baffled. She was sure it was No 8. When Miss Sanderson, her tutor gave her instructions, she told her so. And now, here she stood outside No 8 but it wasn't an ordinary building at all! It was a church...

Tall spires shooting out of its roof, old stone walls crumbling in parts, red and white roses swaying in the breeze and a big Hydrangea plant standing proudly in the far corner, its pink flowers bowing to the wind.

For a moment she stood there, hesitating, then all of a sudden she rang the bell.

Jacqueline Woodcock, shuttled down the corridor. "Miss O'Brien, Miss O'Brien." she greeted, and without giving Jennifer time to answer, she scooted back along the corridor, her big bottom wobbling away as she led her into Henry's office – Henry waiting anxiously to show off his stake.

"Good morning, Miss O'Brien," he said as he stood up. "Hope you found the place alright, from the directions Miss Woodcock sent you."

A big beefy man with broad shoulders and whiskers to match, he spoke with an air of authority.

"Yes Sir. Yes," she acquiesced, not wishing to mention the shock she'd had when she found out it was a church.

"And now Miss O'Brien, we must make a move."

He started from the entrance lobby. "This is the entrance lobby," he asserted, "and the Common Room where my boys and girls frolic, rest and horse around," in fact, they were not boys and girls, but men and women, "and sometimes my staff join in too."

Jennifer's eyes widened. 'Staff frolicking with clients?' she thought.

"Opposite are the toilets," he brushed in by her and then swiftly moved forward. "The Tea Bar," he announced, as Jennifer's eyes followed his directions: a semi-circular bar; a small instant hot water tank standing next to a sink, calling for someone to pull its lever; a large kettle; lily-white tea-cups; saucers; tea-plates; sugar bowls; knives; spoons, all stacked so neatly in piles, as it they hadn't been touched for days.

"The Tea Bar," he asserted, "where my boys and girls serve tea."

Next, was the kitchen. Sparkling white cupboards hung above, shimmering clean utensils neatly laid below They were so neat, you would have thought Hygena had just installed the lot.

He shifted forward. "The Makaton Room," he continued, "where my boys and girls learn to read and count. And here is the Needlecraft Room." he added.

In the far corner, a sewing machine stood proudly; an assortment of threads and balls of wool. Fragments of cloth and half-finished pieces filled the room; half-opened drawers jammed pack with needles; scissors; odds and ends and all sorts of bric-a-brac lay in waiting.

He picked up a scarlet-red jumper and held it in front of his chest. "One of my girls made this," he chuckled and laughed so loudly, the walls were about to crack.

"And this Miss O'Brien, is the Art Room." He shifted again. "My boys and girls excel in Art, you know. Look!" he said, lifting up a couple of unfinished pieces – a man with two faces and a pony with a man's face and no tail, stared at Jennifer from the paintings. She felt queasy, took a step back, but quickly braced herself and moved forward behind him.

He led her to the Computer Room – two well-used computers stood side-by-side on a long desk. Jennifer wondered if any of the clients had the ability to work computers. She guessed, the staff may have been making good use of these, but she didn't say a word.

"And finally Miss O'Brien, the Music Room. Here, my little ones learn the art of music." He ran his finger along the battered piano and … 'zing' … it went, way out of tune. He picked up the guitar and started strumming… 'bang, bang… bang, bang…' it hissed, Jennifer having a job to keep her face straight.

"There is the garden, of course, Miss… Some of my boys are very good gardeners. You are quite welcome to join in any time, if you wish."

"And that's it, Miss O'Brien. If you will come with me to my office, I will give you some timetables and literature of the work we do here."

He wanted to take her around himself, show her what he had achieved at Hope and now he'd done that. He felt proud. But time was running out, so he sped down the corridor as fast as his legs could carry him, Jennifer struggling to keep pace.

"Here's the timetable and some other literature, Miss… I believe you will be staying with us for six weeks. I hope your stay will be a fruitful one," and with that he led her straight to the door.

Henry Brockenhurst, had a meeting to attend.

Jennifer O'Brien, went into the Common Room to look at the papers and make some notes on what she'd just seen.

She pulled out the papers, had a quick look at them, and stuffed them back in her bag. Then she fished out the timetable and started reading it:

Monday -	10am	Mat Bowls
	12-2pm	Lunch – own packed lunch
	2.30pm	Makaton
	4pm	Tea
	4.30pm	Home
Tuesday -	10am	Mat Bowls
	12-2pm	Lunch
	2.30pm	Needlecraft, Gardening, Music, Cookery
Wednesday -		Day Off
Thursday -	10am	Trips, Horse riding
	12-2pm	Lunch
	2.30pm	Arts, Music, Gardening, Cookery
	4pm	Tea
	4.30pm	Home
Friday -	10am	Computing, Gardening, Music, Makaton
	2pm	Home

Jennifer looked at the timetable again then tucked it in her bag.

Today was Induction Day. She had six more weeks there to observe, study, partake and record a project as part of her finals for her Nursing qualifications. There was a lot going on – she could see that. So she would come early on Monday morning, pen and paper ready.

Only, she didn't know that the greatest show on earth could not have prepared her for what she was about to witness…

CHAPTER TWENTY-SEVEN

With Miss McCorkindale having died suddenly, the movement of her inmates out of Mercy Farm into new places of residence, wasn't going to be that easy. New homes had to be found for all 15 women and that was going to take some time, take some doing; a drain on the already stretched resources.

The task of finding placements for all 15 residents was given to Susannah Denton and since a lot of changes had taken place, now that she was a Social Worker, it meant she had to handle her job differently.

She had to check out credentials of these new placements, make several visits, fill out forms, file Reports and get them signed and counter-signed by a hierarchy of professionals, before she could place a client in a new home; a mountain of paperwork about which she was not too happy.

Times had certainly changed.

Meanwhile, life at Mercy Farm had to continue and Mam's Manager, Delia, did her best to carry on in her tradition.

Attending Hope Centre was a priority for 'the girls' for it was there that they were supposed to learn most of their skills, learn to develop a community spirit, limited or partial, though it may be. So, as regular as clockwork, the girls made their journey to Hope Centre in Hope's Minibus; some attending daily, others two or three times a week; some looking forward to it, others not too keen.

It was 9.30am that morning when Trixie and the others arrived at Hope Centre. Someone had tampered with the van (Percy, a resident – they were sure) and it took a while for Hugh, the driver, to put it right.

But back at Hope Centre someone was waiting.

Damien Featherstone, followed the instructors to the van. It was late. Thirty years old or so, six foot tall, with a tanned body, broad, burly shoulders and strong arms to match, Damien brushed forward and stood at the bottom of the steps, eyes as blue as marbles and blond hair fluttering with the wind. He looked like a cross between Marlon Brando and Spartacus – so handsome that they nicknamed him Spartacus.

As the women drifted out of the van, Spartacus's eyes caught sight of Trixie's cute face. Their eyes met. He moved one step closer, held Trixie's hand with a firm grip and led her slowly down the van's step, straight through to the Common Room. Something clicked! And from that day onwards they never drifted apart – both holding each other's hand; he following her, she him, almost everywhere they went.

Jennifer's pen clicked… she started taking notes…

Spartacus was a man who loved the outdoor life. And when he was allocated to gardening, he took it on with pride. He planted everything he was allowed to: lettuce, tomatoes, carrots, cucumber, pumpkin and even had a go at water melons. But his pumpkins thrived and thrived.

Trixie on the other hand tried to improve her notes on the guitar and was doing very well with her cookery classes, especially baking. Then one afternoon at Makaton class, Spartacus got into one of his tantrums.

Hugh, the instructor, picked up a card and looked at Spartacus. "Man," he said, pointing at a drawing on the card.

"W-a-a-a-nn!…" Spartacus went, swinging his head from side-to-side, as he tried to get the word out.

"No, Man," Hugh asserted.

"W-a-a-a-n-n…" Spartacus strained, his temper rising, as he tried to spit the word out. Then… thump! he hit the card lying in front of him.

Trixie jumped to her feet and held his hand.

"N-a-ah, N-a-ah," she coaxed.

"No. No. No!" Hugh went, and… 'Wham!' Spartacus put his head on the desk, banged it with his fist, stood up and with two giant leaps forward, he went straight out the door.

Trixie scrambled to her feet and rushed out behind him, "…come on," she went, "… on," she coaxed, then, after a few minutes of coaxing, his temper eased, and she succeeded in bringing him back in class to learn Makaton.

Trixie was the only one it seemed, who managed to calm Spartacus. No-one else had ever been able to do that before. And Jennifer O'Brien scribbled on…

The days went by and Trixie and Spartacus got closer and closer. Not only were they holding hands, they started pecking each other on the cheek – holding hands, pecking, pecking – but nothing more. Whether they knew about sex or whether it was firmly planted in their heads that sex was forbidden, no-one ever knew. But they were inseparable – she 'the dumbbell, he, the bronze and handsome Mongol' the one they called Spartacus.

Meanwhile, Spartacus's pumpkin was growing so large, that Hugh said it was time to pick it. So the next day Spartacus picked the pumpkin and landed it, 'plunk,' straight on Trixie's kitchen table.

Trixie was delighted.

"A-a-a-h"… she went, "-ake"… meaning, she was going to make a cake with it.

And so with the help of Sandra the instructor, they sliced the pumpkin, grated a few pieces and mixed it with butter, eggs, flour and sugar, she had already beaten. Then she added the spices and raisins, scooped it into the baking tin and into the oven it went – the smell of the spices wafting all over the building – the result, a whopping big 5lb pumpkin cake.

"A-a-a-h," Trixie went, when she saw her cake, her face bubbling with joy. She let it cool, then she and Sandra started slicing it.

At teatime she took two slices, wrapped them in napkins and took them in to Spartacus, where he was having his tea in the Tea Room. "-ook," she announced, "-ake"… "ake"… she enticed, unwrapping the pieces and handing them to Spartacus – its aroma was hard to resist.

By the smell of it, Spartacus knew straight away that it was made from the pumpkin he had given her and his face came alight. He sprung to his feet, hugged her and announced, "T-i-x-i- m-m a-ke 'um-k-i-n - 'ake"…

"Trixie make a pumpkin cake," the others joined in. They stood up and "Hurray," they went, and then sat down abruptly again.

That day they had a feast of pumpkin cake for tea. Everyone had a slice of Trixie's pumpkin cake and its intoxicating smell prompted them to ask for more, and more…

They didn't stand in line. They didn't tow the line. No-one queued. They just moved forward, one here, one there, on they went, each being served in a totally disorganised fashion. It was like a scene from McDonalds – no-one queuing, yet everyone getting served. Mayhem! As Trixie's heart bobbed away, she dishing out her pumpkin cake.

They ate, they drank, some horsing around, others slapping each other on the back; some cracking jokes and the staff joining in at times – in and out of the toilet they went – then Phillipa came out of the toilet, eyes red as a beetroot. They began to swell.

Shocked, she was crying, silently… someone had assaulted her – but no-one was speaking.

It happened quite often this assault – to different clients, at different times, but no-one dared talk… silence… hush, hush… it was like a secret code that no-one dared to break.

No-one dared investigate.

Jennifer O'Brien looked on in awe. It was as if she was on a different planet; a different world. But she wasn't. She was here, right here on earth, witnessing a spectacle, a scene so bewildering…

Her mind boggled as she scribbled on…

CHAPTER TWENTY-EIGHT

Jennifer O'Brien looked at her programme... Tuesday - - 10am... Mat Bowls. It was a relief. After the experience of last week, she was looking forward to Mat Bowls.

Hope's van arrived promptly at 9.30am to take them there. Tall trees dotted here and there on both sides of the road, its branches swaying with the wind; a house here, a house there. Off they glided, the van swerving and diving at corners to avoid the huge traffic jam. It managed to get there on time.

Jennifer watched, pen and paper in hand, as each client headed straight to the cloakroom, paid the attendant, hung their coats up, changed their shoes and made for the Bowling Room. They acted just like any normal person would – then the games started.

Two instructors stood on each side of the room behind a cluster of chairs and a table, leading them on.

Gwendoline went first.

"Come on Gwen, come on Gwen," and... s-w-i-r-l-l... the ball tumbled forward and knocked over one pin. "Hurray, for Gwen. Hurray!" they went, Sandra's voice towering above the others while Hugh was taking scores.

Terry was next. "On wit Terry, on wit Terry," and... s-w-i-i-l-l... the ball tumbled forward and two pins went over. "Terry es firs, Terry es firs," they shouted. "Two for Terry, Two for Terry..." they hollered. On and on they went.

Then it was Trixie's turn. "Come on Trixie, come on Trix," she could hear them yelling.

Nervously, she stepped onto the smooth, polished floor, picked up the ball between fingers and thumb and... w-i-z-z-z... the ball rolled to the side and did not reach the end.

"A-a-ah," they went. "No score! No score!" then a voice bellowed way above the others. It was Sandra's.

"Shall we give Trixie another try?" she yelled.

"Yeah, yeah, yeah, yeah," they rallied, altogether as if in tune.

"OK Trixie, off you go."

Bracing herself, Trixie bent over, and holding the ball firmly between fingers and thumb, S-w-i-r-r-l-l... it skidded forward and knocked four pins over.

"Trixie in, Trixie in," they hollered...

Then, "Whoopee, wha hoo, hey, hey!" it was Percy's voice - - and...

"On with Hope, Hope! Hope! Three for Hope," they chanted, Trixie's face beaming as she put up two fingers. She still couldn't get it right. She just couldn't count.

At last it was Spartacus's turn.

"Come on Spartie. Come on Spartie," they bellowed, Sandra's voice straining above the others.

With precision, Spartacus moved forward straight onto the edge of the shiny, polished floor. Strong burly arms, skin as tanned as horses hide, he bent over, strands of blond hair dangling over his forehead as he picked up the ball between thumb and fingers, marble-blue eyes fixed on his target and... "WHAM!..." seven pins hurled down in one big sweep.

"Whahoo! Yippee!" They screamed. "Spartacus! Spartacus got de cup. Seven for Hope. Hope for de cup! The cup for Spartacus. Hope get de cup..." On and on they went, whistling, hooting, like loudspeakers... their voices echoing through the shambled building, its walls ready to burst.

In the excitement, Spartacus lifted both arms in the air and started dancing around like an Indian warrior, the two instructors' faces beaming as Trixie joined in.

Then, all of a sudden it went quiet – the noise stopped. Not a sound.

Jennifer sat there, dumbstruck! She wasn't sure if she was in a nuthouse, a Bowling Alley or just on another planet, from another world.

Here they were, these funny people, making all this fuss about 'Hope won the cup, Spartacus won the cup,' but they were not playing against any other team, institution or house at all! No-one was playing against the other – no formal organisation, just haphazardly each playing, one in front of the other, scoring points.

She didn't understand... But that was how it was; that's how the instructors wanted it. Just a day out to have fun and Spartacus had won the day. He was their hero.

Then, to top it all, when she returned to Hope Centre that day, Percy whizzed past her. "We took de cup from West Ham," he spurted. "We licked them... We won de cup! We won de cup!" and he sprinted off.

A few moments later, he reappeared. "Jacqueline got de crown," he chanted. "We won de crown," and, as if ascending into the clouds, he disappeared, clean out of sight.

A tall, lanky man, Percy was immaculately dressed in his dark suit and brown tie. He looked normal, like any other being, but he was nuts alright... batty as a fruitcake.

There was plenty for the bewildered Jennifer to record as she went home that day, thinking of the weird and mysterious world she had just been part of...

CHAPTER TWENTY-NINE

Spartacus hardly had time to get home that day, when Henry Brockenhurst phoned his family and told them all about how Spartacus had won the day – Spartacus was their hero. And so, that evening at suppertime, Wally, his brother was ready and waiting for him.

Wally hated Spartacus – envied his good looks, his bronze body, his charm with the ladies; for Wally was the opposite. Thin and lanky, a hooked nose, jet black hair and black slimy eyes to match. Women kept their distance from him.

Just as Spartacus was about to put the first mouthful of food into his mouth, Wally started. "Ah hear you knocked them pins down eh. What's the matter; arms went floppy, did it?"

"Stop it Wally!" his mother butted in.

Wally twisted his mouth – then went silent. But Wally couldn't keep silent for long. He couldn't resist taunting Spartacus.

"…I… loss the strength, did it? Dem chunky arms went straw eh… couldn't chuck another of dem pin down… ha, ha ha!…" he laughed.

"Stop it Wally! I warn you."

Spartacus swallowed. The place went silent, then…

"Ah hear dem goofy women went crazy… and… what you call her… that Trix-a-ma-do…"

Crash!… Spartacus picked up his plate of food, crashed it against the wall, banged his fist on the table and stormed out – big heavy strides, one foot in front of the other. Like a giant he moved, stark raving mad, the rain pelting down on his shoulders.

No-one moved. They knew full well, that when Spartacus went into one of his tantrums, he was best left alone. All they could do was leave the back door ajar and hope he would soon come in.

Spartacus headed straight for the shed. He butted, lashed and kicked the sandbag, boxing, boxing... furiously. So furious, he was, he didn't hear the outburst of thunder roaring its head outside. "Thump! Thump! Thump! Thump!" he hammered, waging into the sandbag, then, 'Bang!'... a loud crackling noise as lightening struck and Spartacus slumped onto the floor, dead!

Next morning, Trixie arrived at Hope Centre, happy as a lark. She had her man, Spartacus and she was happy. So happy she was, she didn't even notice the silence that clouded the place. But then, when she tried to make contact with Gwen, Gwen walked away.

Everywhere she turned, they seemed to evade her. Then, Henry Brockenhurst sent for her.

When Trixie entered his office, she found Sandra sitting next to him, a cloud hanging over their faces. Her face dropped. Then Sandra began.

With Makaton and finger signs, Sandra went on and on, until finally, she managed to get through to Trixie, that Spartacus was dead!

"N-a-a-ah... N-a-aah... N-a-a-ah..." Trixie screamed. She cried and cried and they couldn't stop her.

Her grieving went on for days on end, as she tried, in her Mongol mind, to fathom out what had happened. Day after day - - - no Spartacus. Then, suddenly one day she stopped crying.

Henry Brockenhurst didn't get over the shock for a long time. If only he had a crystal ball, he would have seen that in a few years time, Hope Centre would be closed forever. And none of his protégés would get a job in the outside world either.

Henry's vision was too narrow.

He had trained them to eat together, sleep together, play together, work together and even travel on a separate bus together. Never really teaching them to mix with the outside world… if only…

Henry's dream was lost forever.

Jennifer O'Brien had lots to record… in her final project for her Nursing registration.

She'd scooped dynamite; she would come up trumps, she knew that. With a little more academic might, she would get an A, or better still, Excellent!

Jennifer O'Brien was certain to pass.

But for Trixie, the same could not be said.

Tried as she did, she couldn't stop brooding.

She had lost her man, Spartacus. The only man she had ever loved, gone! Lost forever!

And so, once again she was left all alone in the world – left to the mercy of the indomitable Frankie and Jonnie, where something more sinister awaited her fate…

CHAPTER THIRTY

It was February 1988, almost a year now since Trixie had moved into her new home at the Mill and she was settling in nicely.

A mixed bunch of residents they were. There was Jessica, Clarissa, Marj, Martha, Colleen, Gemima, Trixie, her best friend Patsy and of course, Frankie and Jonnie had moved in too.

An all-female group. All ten of them were mentally retarded, or Mongols, as they were sometimes called.

Mrs Rafferty the owner was a kind, caring and motherly lady. She was a trained nurse and believed firmly in feeding and clothing her residents, keeping them warm and comfortable, tending to them when they were sick and giving them lots of love and affection; the same as she would her own children.

She was not a Social Worker and had no time for Social Work theories and methods. Behaviour Modification and Group Therapy, she considered a waste of time. "Such claptrap! Only dogs were given behaviour training," she once confided in a friend.

"Give them lots of love and watch their little hearts mellow," she used to say. And freedom? Well, she certainly allowed them a lot of that.

They used to go out shopping, go to the theatre and on excursions too. And sometimes Mrs Rafferty would supervise them if she thought it was necessary.

What, with Patsy being childlike and Trixie motherly and caring, it didn't take long for them to become friends. They soon stuck together like glue and one day they decided to go to the theatre to see Cinderella and Trixie returned home ecstatic.

"Sip-per-s! Sipp-er!"… she kept on chanting, referring to Cinderella's slippers and they all laughed their heads off. They thought she was going off her rocker.

Then, one evening, they were watching 'Remembrance Day' on the television and to watch their behaviour was a pantomime in itself.

Trixie wasn't well, so she tried to go off to her room to have a little rest. But Patsy wouldn't let her. "Come on! Come on! You miss it!" Patsy was trying to entice her, but to no avail.

Then, all of a sudden, Jessica went, "Ohh!… it's Adelaide!" And…

"The pipes, The bandsmen!" Clarissa butted in, as the Scottish guards marched in, their colourful tartan skirts fluttering in the air, as they lifted their feet one at a time and marched swiftly forward. They were blowing their pipes with style and the other ladies joined in the chorus.

They watched with interest, then, with precision, the Sergeant Major appeared. He stood to salute, issuing commands to his men and Marj put her hands to her ears and went, "Ooooh…!" as if to say, 'too much of that man. I am scared of him.'

After a short while, Trixie reappeared and Patsy was happy to see her. She got up and kissed her on the cheek, both hugging, kissing the other, Patsy drooling. "Oh Look! She loves me. She loves me. Go on! She loves me," and Patsy was blushing.

An odd bunch of creatures they were.

Jessica, the stubby one, had a moon-shaped face and dark, curly hair on a large, round head. Whilst, Clarissa was tall and lanky, with a thin face and long straight hair, which hung around it like wire.

Marj on the other hand looked small, but she was well proportioned, with black hair and a rather sheepish look. She tended to wander into people's rooms at night and scare the hell out of them. Mousy-haired Colleen, though lean was chesty and not of robust health. The slightest mishap tended to set her off, crying and coughing. Then, there was Martha, the oldest of the lot. At 75, they saw her as 'The Maharaja,' but they called her Marda, a nickname which stuck.

Trixie's best friend, Patsy, was short, fat and dumpy, with straight stubby black hair bobbed around her cupid-like face. She was very childish and would wimp at the simplest disturbance, crying like a little child would.

Frankie, Jonnie and Trixie were not new characters to the scene. Their place was already set. But Gemima was a star.

Tall and auburn-haired, she had the features of a Goddess. She always dressed immaculately, had hazel eyes and a face exquisitely chiselled. She used to stand in front of the mirror for ages, grooming herself to perfection, before she went out. But Gemima was the most disturbed of the lot. When she tried to speak, her words always came out the wrong way out.

Funny, isn't it. Here they were, mentally retarded, yet able to express their feelings for each other so well at times, with no strings or conditions attached. Indeed they followed the programme with interest and made comments, just like any other group of women would.

One day, Colleen and Marj had an argument. Marj had wandered into Colleen's room during the night and Colleen went mad. She refused to sit at the same table as Marj and shouted at her.

"Go on. Get off with you," she bawled and Marj started to cry, saved only by Josie's intervention.

"Leave her alone Colleen," Josie intervened. "She is entitled to sit here and have her breakfast, just like you." And Colleen too started to cry. She was bawling her head off.

"At school is de same ting. Always de same ting…" Colleen sobbed, both women bawling their heads off. Like two little kids, they were sobbing their hearts out and Josie was at a lost to know what to do.

Strange isn't it. One minute they were acting normally and the next they were like children. 'So what is mental illness? And where can the line be drawn?'

Mental health, it is believed, is the ability to play the game of social living and play it well. So, if a person plays it badly, like Marj and Colleen were doing, does that mean they were mentally ill? What then, is the difference between social non-conformity and mental illness?

As far as the behaviour of these two was concerned, it does not seem to lie in observable facts, but in people's attitude towards them. If we cannot communicate with certain types of people, we then consider them inferior and refer to them as mentally ill, mad, crazy or insane.

The pattern of behaviour that these women displayed, was very similar to how any normal group of women would behave. They fought, they quarrelled, they cried, they loved, like most so-called 'normals' would. Only, their behaviour was a little naive at times. And in the midst of it all, was Trixie, giving her love to anyone she liked. Naively, yet astute in her own kind of way.

Christmas soon came and the behaviour of the women at The Mill was no different to any other group of women.

It was freezing cold outside, the ground covered in almost two inches of snow and Josie arrived in a thick, red fur-lined coat, looking like Father Christmas himself.

"Father Christmas is a little late in coming," she declared, as she entered the front door, shivering.

When Trixie saw her, she didn't waste any time. She helped her unbutton her coat, and then she took her handbag from her gently.

She could see Josie was cold and she was doing her best to help her. As if to say, 'Oh you are so cold. Let me help you.'

She gave her a little peck on the cheek and continued unbuttoning her coat, then she took it and Josie's handbag and hung them safely on the coat stand, where the staff's belongings were kept. Josie was quite taken aback.

It was her way of showing Josie she cared, telling her she liked her and that she wanted her to stay. For, she couldn't speak properly, so she demonstrated her love through action.

Josie then went to the kitchen to make a hot drink and Gemima appeared and handed her a Christmas present. It was a tin of Yardley's talcum powder.

"Ah do… you like…" she tried to say, handing the gift over. "Ah you wan'… a 'ave it,"… she stuttered and Josie took it. But a sad shadow came over her face. She was in tears.

She couldn't hold it any more. She burst out crying and told Josie all about how Frankie and Jonnie were treating her so badly.

Gemima, who was considered odd, used to wash the same dish at the kitchen sink, over and over again. She loved gardening, but she would weed the same patch over and over, until she worked herself to a pitch.

A strange lot they were, these women at The Mill. But like a jigsaw puzzle, they fitted together, in an odd sort of way.

Most of them really liked Josie. She only had to ask and they would do anything to try and please her. And there was one favour she wanted. She badly wanted a photo of them for her family album.

After tea, they were gathered in the living room watching TV, when she entered.

"Come on. Let's take a Christmas snap," she coaxed and she didn't have to say anymore.

Like little puppets, they lined along in front of the Christmas tree. "Cheese!" she declared and they grinned away, as she clicked… and clicked… another photo to stick in her family album, to remind her of the days gone by.

An unusual mixture, they were; sometimes mad, sometimes sane; sometimes glad, sometimes sad; sometimes normal, sometimes childlike; a group of women behaving

149

like any other bunch would, only in a naive and unconventional way.

But two persons were missing from that photograph. They were Frankie and Jonnie.

Frankie and Jonnie were green with envy, purple with hate. They didn't like the way certain residents were getting so much attention and they were determined to do something about it.

But they had to bide their time, plan their actions carefully, before they could make their next move.

CHAPTER THIRTY-ONE

1988 was certainly a year to remember. For, in October that same year, Trixie also celebrated her 43rd birthday and she felt really good.

Though The Mill was an institution: all 10 inmates eating their meals at the same time; their beds made at the same time; and their laundry washed together at the same time, Mrs Rafferty tried to make it as homely as she could. She always gave them a special treat on their birthday and Trixie's was no exception.

When the time came nearer, Josie kept teasing her. She kept on saying, "It's your birthday next week, Trixie," and she would tickle her in the ribs and Trixie would chuckle with joy.

Then, the big day finally came on October 17th, Trixie's 43rd birthday. A day they were to remember for the rest of their lives.

They had nearly finished their breakfast that morning when Josie appeared, her face alight, holding a parcel in her hand, which she hid behind her back.

"Happy Birthday to you…" she sang to Trixie, the others joining in.

"Happy Birthday to you…" they sang together, and… Josie handed Trixie the parcel.

Trixie held the beautifully wrapped package in her hand, looking at it tentatively at first.

She was curious; she was nervous; she was anxious; then, slowly she began to unwrap the package while they egged her on, "Go on! Trixie. Go on!… Open it…" they were shouting.

"Happy Birthday to you!" they sang and you could hear Patsy straining at the top of her voice while Josie lead the chorus, as Trixie continued to unravel the parcel.

Bit by bit, she stripped the paper, until all of a sudden, there it was – a lovely pair of black leather shoes appeared from beneath the folds and layers of paper.

It was her 43rd birthday present.

"Ha! Ha!... A pair of dirty old shoes," Frankie intercepted maliciously, laughing her head off. And by the same token, she went, "Happy Birthday to you..." Jonnie joining in, not really to celebrate, but just to be part of the circus.

Frankie and Jonnie were green with envy and jealousy and so, like a couple of spoilt kids, they tried to disrupt the party. They hustled; they jostled; they sang out of tune; anything they could think of to spoil the fun, but the party continued unabated with Josie butting in when necessary, and the others singing at the top of their voices.

Trixie looked at the shoes, her heart filled with joy. She was hugging it, clinging to it and not wanting to let it go.

"Oh look! Its shoes!" Patsy declared, as if she'd only just woken up to what was happening. But the others continued singing away as if they were at a hen party itself.

Nothing was going to spoil their fun. Then all of a sudden, Martha rushed over and hugged Trixie for three solid minutes, and then one by one, they followed suit.

Trixie was so happy, so excited, she rushed over and gave Patsy a great big kiss, smack on the lips and Patsy chuckled with joy.

"My birthday is April... de same as de Queen Moder," Patsy declared, a huge grin on her face and they all roared with laughter.

Trixie was ecstatic and the kissing went on for a long time, it seemed. Then slowly, piece by piece, she began fishing out the padded pieces of paper from the shoe box and handed it to her friends.

" 'Ere you are," she said, not really aware that they were pieces of paper.

In her retarded mind, she believed that they were parts of her present and so she was happy to share them with others. For, that was the kind of woman Trixie O'Connor was; a kind, caring, all embracing person, ready to share with the world, whatever she had.

Later that day, they went through the same charade with her birthday cake; blue icing over sponge with 43 candles. Puffing and blowing, hugging and kissing. Singing and chanting, they carried on and by evening they had almost demolished the whole cake.

Trixie O'Connor was a very happy lady. She was almost brimming over with joy.

As for Frankie and Jonnie? Well, they were seething with hate, envy, jealousy and anger. They were almost boiling over with hatred.

"Did you see how dey pamper 'er kissin' 'er dey was," Frankie blurted out, storming into the bedroom she shared with Jonnie.

"Ye-ah!… And expensive shoes she got too," Jonnie added to Frankie's cursory remarks.

"Well, we go see to dat!" they both uttered together, determinedly.

That night, they held their breath. They watched and waited till everyone was asleep, then they saw Trixie on the landing.

Suddenly, as if from nowhere, Frankie appeared. With lightning speed, she raised her hand and pushed Trixie over, but Trixie screamed and held on as fast as she could. She did not fall over.

Josie heard the scream and rushed across, but Frankie had already disappeared and dived for cover. She was in bed, clean out of sight.

Josie went mad. But as an experienced carer, she knew she had to bide her time; wait for the right moment (a time when they least expected her to) then approach Frankie and

Jonnie. Only then would she be able to have them at her mercy; squeeze the truth out of them, if she must.

That night she didn't sleep well. At 7'o clock the next morning, she was up, sharp. She hammered at their door. "Be down in the kitchen at 8am girls," she instructed.

They were so pleased she'd called them; they thought they were getting a treat. So they came down sharply at 8am, as brazen as two cunning foxes.

But she was waiting.

She took them to the back room and addressed them, one at a time.

"You are evil," she barked at Frankie. "You bully the residents; you beat them up; you pushed Martha over and broke her arm; you gave Marj a black eye; you tried to push Trixie over and you had the gall to say you didn't do it."

Frankie went numb.

"You are a liar and a thief." Josie was raging.

Frankie went mute. She couldn't utter a word. It was as if lightning had just struck her. Like a person who had just been spoken to by a demon, she stood there motionless, shaking all over. She knew she had been caught out and she feared the repercussions.

She just couldn't stop shaking.

But Josie didn't stop there. In the same tone, she had Jonnie in the back room and repeated the same accusations, straight at her.

Jonnie too, went mute. Like a windswept leaf, she stood there helpless, shaking all over. She just couldn't move.

That evening, as Josie was preparing supper in the kitchen, Frankie appeared in the doorway, a guilty look on her face.

"Ah sorry Josie. Ah sorry," she bawled. She moved forward and hugged Josie like a puppy-dog. "Ah… Ah… Ah…" she howled, scared, frightened, that Josie would tell Mrs Rafferty and she might be removed from that home, The Mill, for good.

"Alright! Alright!" Josie snapped. "You won't do it again, will you?"

"Nah, nah... Nah, nah... Ah won't." Frankie sobbed. Like a child, she was begging now, pleading for forgiveness and Josie could not help but feel sorry for her.

A few minutes later, Jonnie appeared. She pushed a present straight into Josie's hand.

"Take it! Take it!" she commanded and walked away. It was a box of chocolates. She reached the doorway, then turned around, "a'm goin' to de flat upstairs," she blurted. "De Inspector say ah must... Take it. Take it... a'm depress... a'm goin to de flat, de hospital..."

Stunned at her outburst, Josie just stood there for a moment and stared.

'Jonnie always behaved like a squeaky little mouse. And now this?' Josie was bewildered.

But that was Jonnie; the other side of her – her interactions with people, always threatening, if not forceful. She never knew how to use persuasion; always force, threats or bullying. And Josie was going to be no exception.

It was the only way she knew how to barter, even for forgiveness. And that's exactly how she approached Josie. It was the only way she knew how to survive.

Whether Josie did tell Mrs Rafferty, no-one will ever know. But Josie had had enough of Frankie and Jonnie. She threatened to leave The Mill.

Josie was popular with the residents and Mrs Rafferty did not want to lose such an important member of staff. So, she coaxed and cajoled and managed to persuade her to stay.

She offered Josie a big rise, and so, after much deliberation Josie decided to stay.

But the drama at The Mill continued. For, whilst Trixie proceeded to offer love and kindness to the people she cared for, Frankie and Jonnie pursued their plight to destroy her, with a vengeance that had a peculiar but unmatchable ring to it.

Nutty as a fruitcake they were, these two women, Frankie and Jonnie, but in a somewhat strange and weird way.

CHAPTER THIRTY-TWO

Almost a year went by and life at The Mill was progressing well. Then in September 1989, Patsy became ill.

Trixie went into Patsy's room as usual one Monday morning to help her get dressed, but found her still in bed. It was unusual for her to stay there, but she was so ill, she just couldn't get out of bed.

"Ah wan' to go to de toilet!... Ah wan' to go to de toilet!..." Patsy cried but she couldn't move.

Realising that Patsy was ill, Trixie rushed to the bathroom and without much fuss, got the bedpan and slid it gently under Patsy's bottom. And... like a monsoon, zoom!... Patsy rained diarrhoea and urine all over the bedpan.

But that didn't disturb Trixie much. She cleaned Patsy's bottom with the toilet roll, washed her thoroughly and made her comfortable. Then, she rushed down to the kitchen to find Josie.

With gestures, signs and a few partially-spoken words, she managed to raise the alarm. Taking Josie to the phone, making a few noises and pointing at it repeatedly, she somehow managed to relay the message that Patsy was sick and Josie should phone the doctor.

And so, in the end, Trixie got the message across.

Quickly, Josie darted up the stairs only to find Patsy shivering. She was so ill she could hardly speak, and her skin was so hot. She had a rising temperature. She was also sweating a lot.

As quick as a flash, Josie bolted down the stairs and phoned the doctor straight away. Then, she raced back upstairs again and together, she and Trixie used a cool sponge on Patsy and wrapped her up warmly. Then, she went down to the kitchen, made some tea and toast and took it up to Patsy whilst Trixie sitting next to her bed, kept watch over her, a forlorn look on her face.

"Ta-ah, aa-ah! Ta-ah, aa-ah!" Trixie stammered, taking the tray from Josie's hand and with her usual gestures, managed to persuade her that she would feed Patsy.

There was no reason why she shouldn't feed her best friend Patsy. For, she was quite capable of it. She often fed her when she was well, so what was the difference now she was ill?

Josie had no qualms, so she left her to it.

Trixie broke the toast into tiny pieces and putting it one piece at a time into Patsy's mouth, she coaxed, "co-me... onn, 'ere you a-re...!" she continued.

Patsy swallowed, then, "Ah... ah... ah..." she cried, opening her mouth again and swallowing the pieces bit by bit, slowly, slowly.

Little by little, Trixie fed her with the toast and a full mug of tea, until Patsy managed to take the lot, groaning a little in between the hot pain in her stomach causing her much discomfort.

It took a while for the doctor to come, but he came. He examined Patsy and diagnosed urinary infection. He prescribed a course of mild antibiotics and kaolin mixture to ease the diarrhoea. But, apart from that short interval when he was with Patsy, Trixie did not budge.

She stayed by Patsy's bedside, helping Josie to tend her, feeding her, taking her to the toilet, washing her body, changing her, doing almost everything for her best friend Patsy.

Every day, she cared for her, hardly leaving her beside. She even ate her food up there in Patsy's bedroom. And every night, she sat on a chair by Patsy's bedside, tucking her in, kissing, cuddling and coaxing her, watching over her like a mother hen nurturing its chick.

Trixie O'Connor lived in that bedroom for a full solid week.

In the past, she used to open the front door and greet Josie when she came on duty in the morning. But now, she couldn't even be bothered to do that. She just sat there, grieving for her best friend, Patsy, and sometimes she cried too.

For days on end she tended her, cared for her, cajoled her, showered her with love, until after a week or so, Patsy began to get better.

With dedication, she nurtured her and within a few weeks, she was back on her feet again and Trixie O'Connor was so relieved; she was so happy.

As for the staff, well, they were dumbfounded, just watching her. She, Trixie, nursing her best friend Patsy, as good as, or even better than many a professional would. They couldn't believe it.

"When Trixie was 10, the Psychologist concluded that she had a mental age of 5 and an IQ of 40," Mrs Rafferty declared, flabbergasted. "And when she was 18 months old, a mere toddler, the doctor wrote that she would be impaired of social skills for the rest of her life. An imbecile," he decided.

"Look! It's all here, written in her big brown file. Look! It's right here in her Case notes," Mrs Rafferty asserted to Josie, shaking her head in disbelief. "And now, she is demonstrating social skills better than many a professional would."

Mrs Rafferty was dumbfounded.

'If only they had shown more thought, done more for Trixie, she could have been a carer just like Josie was. If only….'

Mrs Rafferty was shaking her head. Again and again, it shook, whizzing with thoughts, thinking, thinking…

'She had done very well and we must show our appreciation,' Mrs Rafferty decided. So she ordered some flowers and the next day, they presented her with this bouquet of pink roses.

"Nightingale! Nightingale! Florence Nightingale!"… they were shouting, as she took the flowers from them.

"Ta-ah… Ta-ah… Ta-ah!" she cried, not because she was sad, but because she was happy, so very happy. It was the most precious gift she had ever received and she was brimming with joy; happier still, now that her best fried Patsy was well again.

Trixie Avril O'Connor, was over the moon.

But in the background, two people were seething. Jealousy, hate, anger and spite, were eating away at their souls.

"You see dat Jonnie? Dey give 'er flowers… flowers…" Frankie yelled, stamping her feet like a frustrated child.

"Ye-ah!" Jonnie replied, "and dey callin 'er Nurse too… Florence Nightingale…. Ha…"

"Nurse Florence… Ha!… Ha!… Ha!"… Frankie went and spat on the floor. "Trixie… Miss Nightingale. Ha… We go put a stop to dat," Frankie raged.

"Ye-ah… We go stop dat. Stop it! Stop it! Now!" Jonnie screamed, whining like a hungry hyena.

"Ye-ah! An I kno' how!" Frankie retorted, stamping around restlessly in the bedroom they shared.

"Ye-ah! An 'ow?" Jonnie intercepted.

"Look 'ere Jonnie," Frankie replied. "Patsy was sick. Is'n she? And she better now, isn' she? But she still weak. Isn' she?"

"Ye-ah. So?…"

"So we go give 'er a push; a big push, rite in front ov' de fast car… an she go dead… an…"

She didn't get to finish the sentence.

"Ye-ah! Ye-ah! Ye-ah!" Jonnie agreed, excitedly.

"An"… Frankie continued to finish her sentence, waving her hands up in the air. "Patsy is Trixie best friend. Is she not?"

"Ye-ah!"…

"Dey do everytin' togeder. Do dey not?"

"Ye-ah!"…

"So wen Patsy is dead… Flatten by de car… Zoom!"…
(she made the sound of a moving car); "we go get Trixie, dat
Florence… dat bich! rite under o'er foot again… rite w'ere
we wan't 'er."

"Huh, huh!… Huh, huh!"… Jonnie laughed, hysterically.

That night they hardly slept a wink. They spent most of
the night planning the murder.

They hatched and plotted; plotted and hatched, until they
got it down to a tee. Only, in their childlike minds they
simply planned it like a child would, every weird detail of it,
until eventually, they agreed on the plan.

They would give Patsy and Trixie a treat; invite them to
go to the corner shop with them to buy a box of chocolate
buttons.

They knew that Patsy and Trixie wouldn't refuse to go.
They would do anything for such a treat. Then, once they got
the two of them on the street and saw the speeding vehicle
heading towards them, Jonnie would give the sign and
Frankie would push Patsy straight under the vehicle's wheels.

"She would be dead… flattened… in a jiff!" (Frankie
laid on the floor, stretched out like a dead woman) just to
prove her point.

"You see. Easy as cheesecake!"

"Ha, ha… Ha, ha"… Jonnie roared. Like a spoilt child,
she giggled hopelessly.

"And"… Frankie continued, wiggling her little finger
now, "we go tell Mrs Rafferty dat Patsy fell over in front of
de movin' car."

"Ha!… Ha!… Ha!…" dey won' catch us dis time," they
both declared, roaring their heads off, almost falling over
each other.

The plot was perfectly hatched. All they had to do now
was execute the murder.

CHAPTER THIRTY-THREE

With Patsy having just recovered and Trixie looking quite strained, plus the residents seeming quite low in spirits, Mrs Rafferty decided it was time to give them all a treat. "Time for a holiday," she said to herself. So, she booked a holiday for all 10 of them and reserved Hope's minibus to take them there.

They were going to Badger's holiday camp on the south coast, for a weekend break and when they heard the news, most of them got excited. "Badgers," they were chanting, Patsy thumping Trixie on the shoulders, both giggling away busily packing their best outfit in readiness for the trip.

Then, the big day came. It was a Friday.

They made their way onto Hope's bus, some climbing up the steps, others hobbling, Martha, just about managed to crawl up, the others waiting their turn chanting, "Badgers! Badgers! Ho! Ho! Ho!"

Happily seated now, they began to sing, "Sally... Sally... Ho! Ho! Ho!... Sally... My old man de dustman, 'ere we come... We are goin' to Badgers... Badgers!... Badgers!... 'ere we come!"

You could hear Patsy straining her voice as she tried to catch up with the others. Then, all of a sudden they stopped for a breather.

In the distance, huge waves tumbled, rumbled in the rough sea, as Hope's minibus cruised along. Then Patsy went,

"Ooh! Look! Is a bird. A big, big bird."

"A-a-ah!..." Trixie replied, curiosity getting the better of her.

It was a seagull.

Suddenly, as if from nowhere, the seagulls swooped, a whole flock of them; their grey and white plumage forming patterns as they dived downwards making the most horrendous noises. Like a bunch of naughty kids, they scooped down, looking for a fish or two, a morsel for their meal.

Trixie looked on amazed, her eyes trailing their every move while the thunderous waves played havoc in the sea and the bus jolted along, unceremoniously.

Every now and then a resident chanted a rhyme, then, without warning, Trixie went, "A-a-a-h!"... pointing at the birds, her face alight with joy.

It was 5pm when they finally reached Badgers Holiday Camp and after having their tea, the residents settled in nicely for a good night's sleep. They were very tired from the 4 hour journey and most of them slept well that night.

The next morning Patsy and Trixie decided to go shopping. They couldn't swim and they didn't want to play mat bowls, so they opted for shopping instead.

They headed for the few secondhand shops that littered the town and after much foraging and a lot of giggling, they managed to pick up a few bargains; knickers, socks, a jumper or two and two brightly coloured dresses.

Strange, wasn't it? Most of the stuff they weren't going to wear anyway, but still, they had a ball rummaging around and buying things they wouldn't use. Then, they decided to go to McDonald's for tea.

"What you havin' Trix?" Patsy enquired.

"A-y-e, a-y-e, a-y-e..." Trixie beamed excitedly, pointing to the double whammy burger a customer was enjoying at the time.

Patsy ordered and gingerly they sat down to two huge burgers and two large cups of coffee, frothing milk over its top. They couldn't eat the lot, so they ate and drank what they could and left the rest, a huge smelly heap on the table, the two them burping and belching with over-stuffed stomachs, as they left McDonalds that day.

They were so full up that they had to miss the great supper which was specially laid out for them that evening. But they didn't mind really, for they had something much more important to look forward to that evening – the 'Grand Finale Badger's Dance.' So they went to their room and had a little rest instead.

That evening, looking a little quirky in their newly bought floral dresses, they made their way to the Ball and joined the others. Then, Patsy went, "Come on Trix, let's go for it."

She held Trixie's had and took her onto the floor, twirling and jigging; the Beatles, Elvis Presley and Frank Sinatra's music blasting in turn in the background, as the band played on; every now and then the bandsmen smiling at these funny looking women, behaving in such a childish and odd fashion.

Jessica and Marj went on the floor.

"Come on old girl." Jessica coaxed and Marj went on, wiggling her odd-shaped bottom while the others called,

"Go on Marj, show 'em," as the bandsmen pounded away; some women were lifting their legs high up in the air; others wiggling their fat bums. Ho! Ho!… Wey!… Wey! they were going.

They were having a wail of a time, all but poor Gemima. She just sat there looking so lonesome. No-one wanted to dance with her, so Mrs Rafferty got her on the floor and had her jigging away.

"D…a…n…ce. N…i…ce… Ni…ce… Dan…ce…" she was struggling to say, as she jigged away, her face alight as if the sun itself had just struck her.

But it was too much for Frankie and Jonnie. They could take no more. Mrs Rafferty had warned them to stay away from trouble, so they kept a low profile. That is, until now.

Now, they were seething.

"Come on Jonnie," Frankie blurted. "Let's show 'em!" and with that she grabbed Jonnie, hauled her onto the floor and they began to dance; dancing slow motion, each holding the other close up, squeezing, hugging, like a pair of lovebirds they were. The bandsmen were so amused, they slowed the tempo.

But most of the others had left the floor. They had had enough watching Frankie and Jonnie showing off.

Frankie and Jonnie danced and danced until they had completely flaunted themselves. Then, they sat down again abruptly, as cool as two cucumbers while Mrs Rafferty watched their every move, ready to pounce on them. But, apart from their exhibition, they didn't take a single step out of line.

The Ball was over. The residents had had a nice time. They were tired now and having already packed most of their stuff, they were determined to have a good night's sleep before their journey back home.

But Frankie and Jonnie were not tired. They had laid low for far too long and having watched Patsy and Trixie enjoying themselves, they burnt with envy.

Now, they were roaring to go. They could hardly wait to put their murder plan into action.

CHAPTER THIRTY-FOUR

"You comin' Trixie, Patsy?" Frankie called while Jonnie stood close by her side keeping watch. They were always together, those two, The dyad, as they were sometimes known. But today they were together for a different reason. Today they had something much more pressing on their minds.

"Ta-ah, ta-ah, ta-ah," '(yes we comin)' Trixie stuttered, as she raced upstairs for their coats.

Frankie had promised them a treat; a treat they would never forget. She was going to take them to the corner shop and buy them each a box of chocolate buttons.

'Chocolate buttons!' Oh how they loved them! They couldn't wait to get their hands on those chocs and they certainly wouldn't refuse such a treat. And so, Trixie scrambled into her brown duffel coat, then helped Patsy into her black mackintosh and both headed for the front door of the home they called The Mill, Frankie and Jonnie already waiting impatiently out on the pavement.

It was 5pm that November's evening, 1989, and outside it was pitch black. Trixie was last to leave The Mill, the cold wind biting into her small body. Patsy, having raced ahead, was standing next to Big Frankie; quite excited.

As Trixie turned around to close the front gate behind her, like a flash, Jonnie made the two-finger sign and… WHAM!… the screeching of wheels of the big truck, it's thunderous noise deafening as it tried to ease its breaks, catapulting down the steep hill at near full speed. It had hit something.

The driver didn't stop. He thought he had hit a hump, so he carried on driving.

In fact, he had hit Patsy.

Frightened out of her wits by the noise, Trixie jumped around, only to see her best friend Patsy lying in a crumpled heap on the road, face down with blood spurting everywhere, Frankie and Jonnie standing there, like two pieces of stone, their guilt-ridden faces frozen.

Frankie had pushed Patsy over and no-one saw her except Jonnie. And now they just stood there, not budging an inch.

Trixie rushed over. She could see blood gushing out of Patsy's eyes, her nose, her ears and her abdomen. From everywhere it seemed while her shattered spectacles lay in pieces, a few inches away.

"Na-ah… Na-ah… Na-ah…" she screamed, and as quick as a flash, she took off her coat, turned Patsy over onto her back and wrapped her with it. Then, she bent over and hugged her, howling… hopelessly, uncontrollably.

Her retarded mind was working ten to the dozen now. She somehow knew she had no time to waste. And so, within a split second, she bolted into The Mill with dabs of blood all over her face and clothes. She dashed upstairs and grabbed two blankets from her bed. Then, she rushed into the kitchen and through Makaton signs, gestures and noises, she managed to tell Josie, the carer, that Patsy had had an accident.

"Blood!… Blood!… Blood!… everywhere," she howled, in her own kind of way. Then, she snatched some tea towels, a cup of water and a teaspoon and darted back to her friend Patsy, lying there lifeless on the road.

She covered Patsy with the blanket, sobbing and bawling, "Na-ah… Na-ah… Na-ah…!" 'Oh God. Don't let her die)' she cried, tears streaming down her grief-stricken face.

She took the towel and pressed it onto Patsy's stomach; 'press and squeeze,' she was pressing and squeezing her ribs now, the only way she remembered, but to no avail – the blood came pouring out.

167

Quickly, she mopped and squeezed around Patsy's eyes and nose but the blood kept oozing out. She took a teaspoonful of water and slowly... slowly... she slid it into Patsy's mouth, but it trailed down the side of her cheeks. Slowly... slowly... she put another one in, but the same thing happened again.

Patsy couldn't swallow. She was dead.

She only had three minutes to save Patsy's life and the three minutes was long gone. Patsy was dead. Stone cold dead.

She threw herself over Patsy's dead body and howled and screamed, screamed and howled, the treacherous winter's storm sucking into her naked arm and her scantily clad body.

Shivering in the dark, she shook like a ball of thunder, but she stayed out there in the cold watching over her best friend Patsy.

Meanwhile, Josie was busy trying to get through to the ambulance people. Something was wrong with the phone line and so it took her a while and by the time she rushed out, Patsy was lying there, stone cold dead!

What a sight! Big Frankie and squeaky Jonnie standing there, as if transfixed; Trixie crying over Patsy's dead body; and apart from them, there was no-one else in sight.

No-one else had witnessed the scene.

"Come on Trix," Josie coaxed, distraught by what she had seen.

Trixie did not move.

"Come on darling," she tried again.

Trixie did not budge.

In the distance they could hear a piercing noise, the alarm, the sound of the siren of the ambulance as it thundered its way to the spot. But Trixie did not budge.

Like lightening, the two men shot out of the vehicle, weaving their way towards the crumpled heap lying on the road.

But Trixie stayed put.

Quickly, they checked Patsy's breathing, her pulse, her heartbeat... Nothing! She was dead.

"Come on love. It's no good," they appealed to Trixie, but to no avail. "Come on sweetie," they pleaded again, and then gently hauled her up onto her feet.

Trixie was in a state of shock. Whether she knew Patsy was dead or not, no-one will ever know. But she was certainly very distressed and pining her heart away.

Now, the Police were there. As if from nowhere, they had appeared. Now, they were busy, asking questions, whispering here, questioning there, and jotting down notes as they went along. Then, after some discussion with the Ambulance men, they lifted Patsy's dead body onto the trolley, placed it in the van and made their way swiftly to the hospital's mortuary for a post-mortem to be arranged on her dead body.

Shocked and tired, Josie stood there hugging the grief-stricken Trixie and trying desperately to console her.

Mrs Rafferty was nowhere in sight. She had gone away on holiday, leaving Josie all alone to cope with the tragedy.

As for Frankie and Jonnie, well they had, long ago bolted; ran for cover when they saw the Police. Now, they were back at The Mill, drinking coffee, eating cakes and having a whale of a time. They didn't seem perturbed.

Like children, their childlike minds didn't seem to absorb the horrific implications of what they had done. They thought it was all just a great big joke.

CHAPTER THIRTY-FIVE

But the Ambulance men didn't. They thought it was an accident and having found Patsy already dead, they concentrated their efforts on trying to shift Trixie away from the scene.

They went away with a lot on their minds. And now back at the Ambulance bay, they were busy talking, talking about this Mongol woman, the one they called Trixie; how she braved it all to try and save her best friend's life.

"A Mongol girl? What a story!" they mused. They didn't waste any time.

They sprung into action and before long the media was hot onto Trixie's trail. The local newspaper didn't waste a second more. It got busy and so the next day its front-line story read:

MONGOL GIRL GAVE THE KISS OF LIFE…
Trixie O'Connor, a little Mongol woman, tried to
save her best friend's life, the only way she knew how.
Braving the cold and freezing elements, in her
scantily clad attire, this mentally retarded woman
gave the kiss of life to…

It was too hot a story. The place was buzzing. They had to sell papers, so they gave it the biggest twist they could think of.

'A mentally retarded woman, risking her own life to save that of her best friend's.' They couldn't let that pass by.

They couldn't afford to waste any more time. So they got busy, frantic, speaking here, talking there, phoning here, ringing there; the place was abuzz with action. And so within days they were onto the 'big fish' themselves – the men responsible for recruiting deserving candidates and dishing out the 'Prince's Bravery Award' to them.

It was all fixed. Not a minute wasted. Trixie O'Connor was to get the Prince's Bravery Award and she didn't know about it at the time.

CHAPTER THIRTY-SIX

Back at the Mill, it was a different story. Frankie and Jonnie had murdered Patsy, but when quizzed by Mrs Rafferty, they said Patsy fell and the lorry ran over her. And since Patsy tended to fall over at times anyway, Mrs Rafferty believed them.

Frankie and Jonnie had got off scot free. They weren't batting an eyelid, it seems. Meanwhile, most of the residents were in a state of shock.

As for the grief stricken Trixie, life for her was unbearable. She had lost her soul mate, her best friend Patsy, and now, through Makaton signs, gestures and the pictures they had drawn, they somehow manage to tell her so.

"Dead! Gone forever!" they affirmed. And so Trixie cried and cried…

That evening, she just couldn't stop crying.

She wouldn't eat, she couldn't sleep, and she wouldn't drink anything. She just kept on crying; wept for weeks on end. Just withdrew and pined away. She'd lost interest in everything. No matter how hard she tried.

They sent for the doctor, but that didn't help either. There was not a lot he could do about it.

"She had to get over it in her own time, her own way," he told Mrs Rafferty. "It was the only way," he assured her, as she led him to the front door that day.

CHAPTER THIRTY-SEVEN

It was April 1990, a very special day. The day Trixie was to get her Award and that evening, Titville County Hall was packed with people.

They came from everywhere; some to cheer, some to stare, some to celebrate and some simply to eat the sumptuous mouth watering grub which was prepared for the occasion.

Trixie sat on the front row as proud as a parakeet her face beaming with joy. With Josie on her left and Mrs Rafferty to her right the remaining seats being taken up by newspapermen, cameramen and TV moguls.

The Hall was packed – ablaze with bright lights shining down from everywhere; from the ceilings, from the walls, like rainbows they hung high above, ready to disperse, to shower their multi-coloured beams at the first signal of action.

Then, the lights dimmed. A shadow walked onto the platform.

Suddenly, it lit up again and like a tongue of fire, its fragments rained down onto the figure of the Prince as he moved forward, multi-coloured sparks gleaming; his blue coat ablaze; his gold-framed cap with its familiar logo shimmering; the seam of his black trousers creaseless; his black shoes polished to such a sheen that they shone and the gold buckle on his belt seemed ready to tell a tale.

"Ladies! And Gentlemen!…"

The crowd went silent.

"We have gathered here today to celebrate a very special occasion…"

There was a hush.

"A special occasion for a very special lady…"

The audience went "Ooh!..."

"A special lady; special, not only because of the very brave act she did, but because of who she is..."

The people went "Aah!..." A few claps, then silence.

"She is special because..." he paused "she is a Mongol."

"Hear! Hear!" they went, followed by a few more claps.

"Trixie O'Connor!..." he announced. "Braved the elements on a cold November's night, risking her own life to try and save her best friend's by giving her the kiss of life, the only way she knew how."

"But!..." he paused. "Trixie O'Connor is retarded. She is indeed a Mongol."

The hall erupted. They clapped and hooted and whistled.

"And!..." he continued, "for those of you who do not know what a Mongol is..." he paused, "it is a person who is born mentally retarded."

They whistled and they hooted.

"But! Nowadays," he raised his voice, "we call it, a learning disability."

A thunderous applause; more hoots and more whistling. Like thunder, the Hall shook with action and almost erupted.

"And now Miss Trixie Avril O'Connor, will you please take the stand to receive your Award."

Trixie blushed. Nervously, she climbed the stairs, slowly... slowly... it was the first time ever that she had faced a real Prince and she shook with fear. But she quickly pulled herself together again, curtsied and took the Award, just like Josie had shown her she should.

She'd rehearsed it well and now she did it almost to perfection.

The rapturous thunder of clapping, hooting and whistling was deafening, as it erupted through the building, it's ceiling almost coming alight as the cameras clicked, lights flashing, its colours, like rainbows, raining down on Trixie as she stood there, stunned.

There she was, standing there motionless; she the pauper, he the Prince; both standing there side-by-side, as she held up the shimmering Gold Badge – the Award the Prince had given her, the Award she had earned – for all the world to see.

'There'll be much celebration in the days to come,' she was thinking, for Josie had explained it all to her. 'Letters, greetings, cards, the media, the TV – all busy, each trying to outstrip the other in an effort to grab the frontline story.'

She could see the headline story now:

MONGOL GIRL GETS THE PRINCE'S BRAVERY AWARD
'Miss Trixie O'Connor, a little Mongol lady, risked her own life to try and save her best friend from dying, by giving her the kiss of life!...'

She was getting so excited standing there, momentarily listening to the applause. Her heart was beating ten to the dozen, as she thought.

'There'll be great feasting tonight too,' Josie had told her so. 'A four course dinner, all laid out: Iced melons or smoked salmon for starters; braised steak cooked in red wine; exotic fruits/peaches, topped with rich frothing cream; rich mouth-watering strawberries and thick cream; and iced coffee and mints to top it all off.'

'But that could wait.'

Her head was swimming with thoughts. Things she wanted to say but just couldn't, because she couldn't talk properly as she was dumb.

She looked for Mah in the audience to share this special day with her. 'Mah... Oh Mah!... Where is Mah?' But there was no Mah to be seen.

Mah had long gone. Died prematurely. Died from poverty and exhaustion. They, society, had abandoned her to a life of misery and doom. 'Those people with large families'... they'd hinted... was their own fault they were poor. They brought it on themselves.'

And now Mah was not here to see Trixie O'Connor, her little imbecile daughter, gain a place in history.

Trixie could hear someone, something, someone, more powerful than any other, whispering in her ears, saying:

'No matter how useless, how broken, how
poor you may appear; you are a gift, a
talent, a citizen with unique contributions
to make. And today is proof of that.'

'If only Mah was here?'

Trixie looked down the front row now. Mrs Rafferty sat there. A proud smile on her face.

'She'd sent her two children to private schools and universities, with the money she had made running two Hostels for Mongol women, so Josie had said. With 10 Mongols at £250 a week each, she was earning a cool £2500.

She had done well and now her son was a doctor and her daughter a lawyer. But Trixie didn't mind. Mrs Rafferty was a kind lady. She'd fed them well, cared for them and given them a proper home.'

Trixie O'Connor never did bear any grudges against Mrs Rafferty. Trixie was a sensitive lady, always thought a lot and now she was thinking…

Her eyes trailed along the second row, to the two Social Workers sitting there with uneasy looks on their faces. They had come early to try and grab the front seats, but the media people had beaten them to it. Now there they were sitting uncomfortably in the second row.

'They had read a lot, too many big books: Social Work Journals, Social Work theories, psychotherapy, and behaviour modification – you name it, they read it. And now they were sitting there, their heads puffed up with theories; – spin! spin! and more spin!'

'They'd written too many assessments, case histories and case notes, all filed away in big brown cabinets. Locked away in the dark inner recesses of the nation's bureaucratic social systems. Files waiting to be fished out, photographed and rehearsed by some new 'spin doctor,' ready to discover some new 'spin' theory.'

'Only, now they'd changed the label. Now mental retardation was given a new name. Now, in the 1990s they called it 'learning disability,' but behind the façade, Trixie was still seen as an imbecile, an idiot, a woman they wrote of as 'useless'.'

'Too busy with spin theories they were, to spot the normal everyday human kindness that Trixie was dishing out; qualities which had earned her this very special day.'

'They, the so-called 'normals,' had put their elderly mothers and aunties in Nursing Homes: drowning in the stench of their own urine, suffocating in their own saliva, their stomachs often churning with hunger pains, because the nurses were too busy to spare the time to feed them properly. They were lucky if they got a card or a visit from their relatives once a year.

And they, the Social Workers were too swamped, too busy to care.'

'But she, the imbecile, Trixie, had cared for her buddy, her soul mate, her best friend Patsy. She washed her when she was sick, fed her when she was off her food and took her for long walks when she was down. She, Trixie O'Connor, gave her love to another, unconditionally.'

'They had got it all wrong, the normals. They'd often messed up their own lives, whist she Trixie, the idiot, the one they branded as 'useless,' had practised random kindness, shown appreciation to others, made efforts to devise acts of caring in a world that was becoming increasingly uncaring.'

'For he who is greatest,
Often chooses that which
Is simplest, to reveal his
True power and glory...'

She, Trixie Avril O'Connor, the mentally retarded woman, the one they called the imbecile, taught them how to love.